Merlot Marriage

Fancy Roberts

Contents

Ophie

A Vegas hangover, plus plane turbulence, equals me reaching for my seat belt every ten seconds, contemplating if I need to make a run for the bathroom to puke my guts up.

I'm not sure how much of the nausea is from alcohol and how much is from the knowledge that, when this plane lands, the timer starts on getting my adult life together. In eight weeks, I'll graduate with my master's and run out of excuses not to decide what I want to be when I grow up.

I suppose twenty-six is pushing it, but really, my prefrontal cortex has only just finished cooking. I'm a baby adult who probably still needs adultier-adult supervision.

I definitely needed it this week.

To my right, Sydney groans, just as hungover as I am. I wasn't sure about having my future sister-in-law crash my last college spring break. But she needed a break from work, and I thought I needed a partner in non-crime. Joke's on me—Sydney could drink a frat boy under the table.

How she managed to drink three of those foot-long margaritas while walking down the Strip without even a single stumble is still beyond me. I drank half of one and could barely keep my eyes from crossing.

"I am definitely going to puke when we get off this plane."

Maybe Sydney isn't as tough as I thought. Her moaned words give me hope that I'm not the least cool person in this group.

I am one hundred percent the least cool person on this trip, but at least I'm not the only one with a hangover from hell.

"Don't be such babies," Cassie says, reaching her fingers through the gap in our seats to poke my arm. "But if I ever suggest a Vegas trip again, I give you all permission to dunk my head in a toilet. Actually, I may do it myself so I can puke in peace."

Beside her, her sister Heather and our friend Morgan groan in agreement from the row behind us. We wanted to combine successfully defending our theses, our last spring break of grad school, and Cassie's bachelorette. Theoretically a great idea. However, based on our current state of being, twenty-six is too old for four straight days of debauchery in Sin City.

"*Ach*, man, my head feels like it weighs a hundred kilos," my other seatmate groans from my left. Philip lets out a deep sigh as he rests his head on my shoulder. His South African accent soothes my frayed nerves, but his warm breath on my neck does nothing for the roiling in my stomach. Neither does the dim memory of two nights ago that I've been avoiding ever since it happened.

"I wish we'd had time for real coffee this morning. Whose idea was it to take such an early morning flight?" Sydney leans her head against the window and closes her eyes. "Wake me up if they come around for drinks."

Blocking out the piercing overhead light, I close mine too, willing myself to lose consciousness. Anything to bring this trip to an end and let me go back to my nice, quiet life.

Correction: my quiet, lonely, anxiety-filled life.

"You smell lekker, Ophie," Philip mutters. "Like flowers and…I don't know." His voice trails off as he nuzzles deeper into my neck. He is always this touchy, I remind myself. No one will suspect anything.

"Are you still drunk?" I whisper, praying that Sydney is asleep and not listening.

He lifts a hand, his thumb and pointer finger half an inch apart. "Little bit."

"How drunk have you been this week? I thought…" I tip my head back, dislodging his from my shoulder. Panic joins the party in my intestinal tract, and I glance down at the seat's back pocket, searching for a puke bag.

He rolls his head to the side to eye me. "Sober enough, yeah?"

Sober enough.

So was I.

Neither of us can use the excuse of being too drunk to remember sneaking away from our friends and showing up at the little chapel on the Strip.

Have I made the biggest mistake of my life?

Philip is still staring at me, his ocean blues disconcertingly close. Instead of answering his implied question, I flip my hood over my head and settle back into my seat, ignoring his adorably rumpled face and hair.

There's shifting to either side of me as Philip lifts the armrest between us and Sydney adjusts her legs. Then my head is pulled down on his shoulder. "Have a nap, liefling. I'll wake you just now."

Blessed unconsciousness takes me as Philip's cologne drifts into my nose.

I spend the two-and-a-half-hour flight home to Portland dozing against his shoulder—too tired to keep my eyes open but too awake to sleep deeply. Philip mutters Afrikaans nonsense above me. I have no idea what he's saying, but the lilting words sound so close to English, it feels like I *should*. Fitting, really, that the blur of our Vegas trip stays surreal until the end.

Like it was all a lucid dream of drinking, dancing, eating, and lying by the pool.

I manage to stay in my detached state until the six of us exit baggage claim into a spring downpour. Even stopping for coffee as we leave the terminal doesn't force me completely back to reality, but it does settle my stomach. A chill wind whips through the parking structure, the smell of rain, exhaust, and piss hitting me in the face as we head to the rideshare pickup point. The cold air dissolves my grip on the fog keeping me from facing my future.

"Thanks for letting me crash your trip." Sydney gives Cassie a hug as we wait. "My feet may never recover, but it was fun." Releasing Cassie, she shuffles back to take her coffee from me. "I really thought bringing only one pair of heels to save space for more outfits was smart."

All of us stop to look down. Thick white socks cover Sydney's feet, shoved into a pair of much-too-big flip-flops she borrowed from Philip. She has the right sock pulled up over her sweatpants, almost to her knee, the left one falling down to her calf. The toes and heels of the fabric are already speckled with wet spots.

Combined with her hoodie, messy bun, and raccoon circles from last night's makeup, she looks as messy on the outside as I feel on the inside.

"I don't know if it was the shoes that were the bigger issue or kicking the concrete pylon," Cassie points out. She and Heather share a look, Heather smirking in the way that's been annoying me ever since she met us at the airport five days ago. If Cassie wasn't such a good friend, I'd have said something already, but I was trying to keep the peace. Sydney declared Heather an uptight asshole whose husband couldn't find her clit and laughed in her face. She's not wrong, but the trip's been a little tense ever since.

Sydney lifts her sunglasses, looks both women up and down, then drops them back into place with a shrug. "That pylon came out of nowhere."

There's an amused snort from beside me as Philip steps closer, blocking the cold wind blowing at my back. I lean back, snuggling into his side to keep warm. Maybe I can borrow a little bit of his constant good humor to finish this trip on a good note. Sydney ignores us all, pulling her purse open and looking inside, searching for something.

"Besides, it's just a toenail—it'll grow back." She stops digging in her bag to raise an eyebrow at Cassie and Heather, then nods her head toward Morgan. "At least I knew the names of all the guys I kissed. Unlike some of us."

As Morgan's face goes beet red, I'm doubly glad no one caught Philip and me after our little—big—adventure. We would never hear the end of it, and the whole point is that no one needs to know. Ever.

"The club was really loud, okay? I swear he said his name was Nigel." Morgan hunches her shoulders, but Cassie pulls her in for a one-armed hug.

"The club *was* loud. And his Australian accent was thick," I reassure her. "We only figured out his name was Michael *after* you left with him, when Philip was talking to his friend Simon."

"Ah, my good friend Simon," Philip teases. "Lovely fellow. Shame about the ears."

Morgan huffs, rocking her suitcase on and off its wheels in an agitated way, and Cassie throws an arm over her shoulder, glaring at us. "Just because you two have an unhealthy attachment that prevented Ophie from getting laid, don't take it out on Morgan. She had to break that dry spell. It was the whole point of going to Vegas."

There's a sharp twist in my stomach, and my cheeks heat at her words. The only reason I'd been glad to have Heather along on the trip was so I didn't have to share a room with Cassie and her constant need to push Philip and me together. Sydney, bless her, doesn't give two fucks about my love life.

Since Morgan and her long-term, long-distance boyfriend broke up about six months ago, Cassie has been on a mission to get her back into the dating world—and laid—ever since. Her ex had been working in Dubai for the last two years, and Morgan had been taking care of herself for too long, according to Cassie. The moment we landed in Vegas, she didn't stop pointing out potential men. Literally. She was halfway to getting her a date with our Uber driver by the time we made it to our hotel from the airport.

Why do happily paired-off people always try and force the rest of us to date? Why can't they just accept that I like my life the way it is and stop trying to make me change things? I have enough Big Life Milestones coming my way—I do not need to complicate that by adding dating or a relationship on top of it. I have Philip. I don't need anyone else. Besides, there is a finite number of decent men in the world, and I'm too busy with grad school to look for that needle in a haystack.

I'm not about to let a man derail my education. Again.

Cassie finally stopped trying to set me up with TJ's friends last year when I threatened to tell anyone she set me up with why she's not allowed to be the designated driver anymore. Anywhere.

Those poor sheep still back away from the fence whenever we drive by in her car.

"We do not have an unhealthy attachment. It's called being friends," I point out.

"A real friend wouldn't cockblock the other." Cassie points her phone at me as a gray sedan pulls up in front of us. She checks the license plate. "This is us."

Heather leans in to verify the driver's name while Cassie rushes over to give me a hug. "Thank you for coming. It was fun, right?" she murmurs in my ear.

I hug her back, careful not to spill my coffee on her. "Yes, it was fun. Mostly. I think we're just too old for this shit."

Cassie looks back over her shoulder to where Heather and the driver are loading her suitcase in the trunk. "Sorry my sister was being an asshole. She misses her kids. And also, you know I'm right. You need to get laid as badly as Morgan does. You shouldn't let Philip pussy-block you."

She steps back and hurries to follow her impatient sister into the car, waving as they pull away. Just as their car disappears, Morgan and Sydney's rideshare pulls up. Sydney gives me and Philip hugs before joining her—she and Morgan both live near the Pearl District, so sharing a car made sense. The knot in my stomach that has nothing to do with being hungover squeezes tighter as my friends—and buffers—leave me alone with the consequences of my actions.

There's been a bunch of recent break-ins at my condo complex, and I jumped at the chance to leave my car at Philip's place, where campus security patrols. Now I'm regretting that no one else lives near enough to him to share a car.

It's the first time we've been alone in forty-eight hours. Nervous sweat breaks out on my upper lip, even though it's a cool spring day. The silence between us is tense and awkward as I finish sipping my now-cold coffee.

I can feel him studying me as I nervously shake the empty cup. With a soft chuckle, he takes it from me, walking away to the nearest trash can.

With nothing to hold on to, my fingers clutch the handle of my suitcase, releasing and clicking the button on top over and over. My focus is glued to Philip's back. The fit of his leather jacket across his shoulders. The way his curly brown hair flops to one side as he leans around a pair of teens to toss the cups.

I don't look away quickly enough as he turns, catching my eye and grinning when he sees me staring. Hands shoved in his pockets, he ambles back, that easy smile and loose body telling me I'm the only one feeling nervous about spending the next twenty minutes together in the back of a car. Or the next eight weeks actively ignoring the rash decision we made.

"Well, Mrs. van der Merwe. Should we go home?"

Philip

I pull out my phone to reread the texts from my family as the other graduates mill around me on the lawn.

Mum: *I'm so proud of you, Philip! I can't believe my baby boy is so grown now.*

The series of crying face and heart emoji following her message is four rows deep, making me chuckle.

Dad: *Well done, son. You finally put your mind to something and saw it through. Now the opportunities that await you are endless. How are the job prospects? Need me to put in a word for you with someone?*

I push down my annoyance at Dad's not-so-subtle reference to my younger days. I'm not going to let him get under my skin today.

My brother's message is a video of him, his wife, and my two nephews holding up a banner with the words "Congratulations, Uncle Flippy" in crooked letters, the finger-painted artwork surrounding it the obvious contribution of my nephews, given the paint covering their hands and cheeks. Volume off, I let the video loop a few times until their genuine excitement for me soothes the pinprick wounds left from my dad's message.

"Phil!" Cassie's fiancé, TJ, wanders over, clapping me on the back hard enough that I stumble forward a step. Wincing at the hated nickname and the blow, I shift out of reach, turning to face him just as Cassie comes bounding over.

"We did it!" She giggles and snuggles into his side. "Can you believe it?" Like mine, her black gown is unzipped, a white dress visible beneath. Her cap is in her hand, the tassel swinging as she moves.

"Wasn't sure I was going to make it at the end there. Those finance finals were a bitch." They wouldn't have been so stressful if I had studied like I intended to, but every time I sat down to study, I'd catch myself scrolling through photos of Ophelia and myself, wondering why she was avoiding me.

When she suggested we get married in Vegas, I assumed she and I were on the same page—that defending her thesis was the turning point, and she was ready to take us off the back burner. Was it a bit bananas to go from best friends to married, skipping the steps between? Maybe. But I've done stupider things with far less thought. And I figured we'd been basically dating for the last two years anyway, so why not?

Apparently, we may have been reading from the same book, but we were definitely not on the same page. Maybe not even the same chapter.

Cassie laughs, the sound more carefree than I've heard from any of our friend group in weeks. Eight, to be exact. Since we all stumbled home from Vegas, hungover and full of bad decisions.

"Where's your better half?" TJ looks around as he asks. Cringing when Cassie elbows him in the gut. "What?"

"I promised Ophie we wouldn't tease them today. Be nice."

She promised Ophie? "Why's that?" My curiosity gets the better of me, and I need to know the story behind that statement.

Cassie looks around, checking to see who's nearby. "Because her whole family is here, and she didn't want them getting ideas. You've met her mom, right? I guess ever since Maggie and Kel got engaged, her mom's been talking nonstop about Ophie being the only single one left. Her dad is convinced she needs to move back to Seattle with them if there's nothing keeping her here." She arches an eyebrow at me, but I'm ready for it—I always am when Cassie is around—and don't react.

Black gown flaring, she turns to gaze up at TJ with a soft smile. Not an expression I see often on her mischievous face. "Besides, today is *our* day."

"Your day?"

TJ grins at her, then looks up. "We're headed to the courthouse after this to make everything official. I told her I would wait until graduation to make her my wife and not one hour more. Got the license a week ago."

My wife is wandering around here somewhere too. Maybe if she hadn't scuttled away after the ceremony, I'd know where. I glance around but don't see her brunette mane anywhere.

"Congratulations, that's awesome." My words taste bitter with jealousy. To cover up my half-hearted well-wishes, I add some other pleasantries while Cassie studies me. Twirling her hair around his finger, TJ drones on about all the benefits he can finally take advantage of once they say "I do."

"You know, if you wanted to stay in the States, you and Ophelia could just get married so you can get a green card."

I stutter over the words that stick in my throat at Cassie's too-casual suggestion. Denial is second nature. Outrage is cliché. Confusion stopped being funny a year ago. My feelings might be legitimate, but our friends stopped wanting to hear it ages ago—no matter how many times I declared I wanted to earn the right to stay here on my own.

Especially now that it's all a lie.

I'm still trying to string together a fully formed thought when a familiar warm hand comes to rest against my back.

"Are you okay?" Ophie's whiskey-brown eyes come into view, the concern in them only making it worse. She steps close, wrapping her arm around my waist, one hand making slow circles across my back.

"Yup. Fine. Never better," I gasp.

Cassie laughs. "I was just telling Philip he should make you Mrs. van der Merwe so he doesn't have to go back to South Africa."

I know she's just being her usual romantic-slash-diabolical self, but seeing Ophie's cheeks turn bright pink at being called "Mrs." does funny things to my stomach. At the same time, my mind grasps for something to say to distract Cassie from her line of thought. Better not to protest too much, or she'll be suspicious.

"Cassie, you promised," Ophie whispers, looking around as if someone might hear her. She moves like a little bird, head darting to and fro, hands opening and closing the embossed leather folio we received on stage with the same nervous energy she clicks her pen when she's past the point of productive studying.

"What did she promise? Not to call you Mrs. van der Merwe?" I tease. Pulling her folio away before she breaks it, I stack it with my own, then give in to the urge to rile her up. It's so easy, I can't help myself. Self-control has never been my strong suit, and when it comes to Ophie, I have almost none.

I glance around but don't see her family anywhere, so I wink at Cassie and TJ before throwing my arm over her shoulder.

The movement knocks her unzipped robe off one shoulder. With a squeak, she grabs at it, but that only sends it sliding farther off her silky skin. I move back to give her space while she wrestles to get the bulky fabric back in place. Her hood keeps tangling with her elbow, and Ophie's grunts of frustration get louder and funnier with each attempt.

"*That*. You know." Even as she fights with her hood, she doesn't quit arguing with me. Naturally, I have to argue back. Especially with an audience eating up our playful banter, their eyes big as saucers.

"I know what?"

"Philip, come on."

"Come on what?" I snicker at my own joke, and Ophie goes a shade pinker. TJ reaches out, and I high-five him as Cassie digs an elbow into his side.

"Gross." Gown straightened, she takes a deep breath but still doesn't meet my eyes. "Don't call me *that*." My girl glares at me, obviously annoyed that I'm playing into Cassie's suggestion, who has no idea that Ophie and I beat her to the altar. The double meaning behind every word of our argument just makes the whole thing more fun.

I haven't had this much fun in *weeks*.

I lean close, tugging Ophie's hood straight over her unzipped gown. The blue dress she's wearing underneath does amazing things to her tits. Not that I'm looking. I swear.

"You're going to have to be more specific, Ophie van der Merwe." I dance back a few steps to avoid getting a swat, her hand whipping past my stomach with enough force that I'm grateful my reflexes are as fast as they are. Her dark hair swings with the movement, the scent of her shampoo wafting back into my nose.

I've been breathing it in for two years, the slightly floral scent drawing me in like a bee to a flower.

The flower in question is glaring at me more like a Venus flytrap than a rose. She stomps the two steps to close the distance between us, lifting up on her toes and jabbing a finger into my chest. "I am not, and I never will be, Mrs. van der Merwe." Her American tongue struggles to roll the *r* properly, but her "Fun der Mer-ve" is as close as most non-Afrikaners can get.

Something playful and wicked breaks free inside my chest at Ophie's vehement denial. So instead of responding, I drop to one knee in front of her.

Gasps fill the air around us.

Cassie squeals, and in my peripheral vision, the milling crowd forms a loose circle around us. Girls I don't know whisper excitedly, tugging on the people beside them.

"Ophelia Moore..." I drag out my words, staring at the hem of her black robe that's now close to eye level. As I look up at her from this angle, her blue dress dancing in the breeze and pink lips parted, the carefully walled off bit of my heart that's kept my love for her designated as strictly platonic slips, and something a little more intense floods in. The strength of the emotion takes me by surprise, and my voice cracks as I speak, ruining the playful tone I was going for. "Will you—"

I'm cut off by an ear-piercing cry of "Ophelia!"

Shit.

Now I've done it.

I grab the zipper pull at the hem of her gown. "—let me zip you up?"

Clearing the unexpected thickness in my throat, I hook the bottom of the zipper together and zip up Ophelia's robe as quickly as I can, pushing up to my feet as I do. Her mom comes barreling toward us, her excited noises getting louder as she approaches.

"Ophie, darling, who's this? You didn't tell us you had a boyfriend."

Making sure of my smile, I turn and wave. "Hi, Jenny."

"Oh." Mrs. Moore stops short, recognition dawning on her face. "Hi, Philip. I didn't recognize you from the back." She waves a hand at the slowly thinning crowd. "All the robes make everyone look the same."

Heat floods the back of my neck at Jenny's dismissal. "No worries. It's nice to see you again." I relax my stance, giving Ophie some space.

"Still playing jokes, I see." Mark steps up beside her, a hand resting on her shoulder.

I shrug. "The opportunity presented itself, and I went for it." Looking around at the dissipating crowd, I catch more than one girl shaking her head in my direction. Ophie's cheeks are still pink, although that could be from the sun. "You knew it was just jokes, right?"

Ophie glares at me, stepping closer to her mom. "Yes. But it was a bad joke, Philip."

"It was, you're right." I shrug. "How are you all? Are you staying for the whole weekend?"

"No, unfortunately, we've got to drive back tonight. I have an important client coming from out of town tomorrow." Dave, Ophie's brother-in-law, joins the group. "Daisy is making her famous lasagna, with pasta from scratch and everything."

"Yes, and it takes all day to cook, so I need to get back early." The eldest Moore sister, Daisy, steps into view, towing her two kids behind her. The preteen boy is glued to the handheld video game console in his grip, while the girl is walking backward, chatting to Kel's daughter, Olive. Kel and Maggie follow, her hands looped over his arm as she navigates the grassy field, the smallest hint of a baby bump outlined by her clothes.

Leaning down, I quickly whisper in Ophie's ear, "God, I forgot how much family you have, liefling."

"And they're all nosy as fuck, so quit being a brat," she whispers back before straightening with a smile.

"Well, Ophie is very lucky to have you all here today. I would have loved to have my family here to celebrate with me. Maybe then my father would believe I actually graduated." I try not to let the bitterness that's been stewing in my gut leak out with my words, but Jenny casts a sideways glance at me, and I know I haven't quite managed it.

Philip

SHOVING OUR CAPS AND balled-up gowns into the trunk of my car, Ophie waves goodbye to her family as they pull out of the restaurant parking lot. "Was the joke about Daisy's meatballs really necessary?" With a true beleaguered sitcom-wife sigh, she slides into the passenger seat of my car.

I grin to myself, waving to Kel and Maggie as they follow the others. "Better than making a joke about Elvis serenading us as he signed the marriage license," I point out as I climb behind the wheel.

Joining the Moores for a celebratory lunch had been equal parts painful and fun. On the one hand, poking subtle fun at Ophie's oldest sister and making Maggie giggle had been a delightful way to spend an afternoon. And once Mrs. Moore forgave me for my joke earlier, she had smothered me with motherly love.

But every squeeze of the shoulder or "that's lovely, dear" was a reminder that my family is thousands of miles away. And of the giant secret we're keeping from all of them.

We head back to my place in silence for a few minutes, and I can't help thinking about how little time I have left.

The familiar panic of "where do I go now?" swirls in my belly, amplified by the silence. Two years felt like forever when I arrived in the States. Now it's almost gone, and the expiration date on my student visa is too close for comfort. Especially since I have no home to go back to.

"Have you heard from any of the jobs you applied to?" Ophie asks, breaking the quiet.

"Some. Most of them aren't willing to jump through the immigration hoops for me, but there are a few potential ones that I haven't heard from yet. What about you? Has the port called you back about the job?"

The setting sun glints off her sunglasses, golden hour approaching as we near my apartment. Ophie stares out the window for a beat before turning to give me a small smile. "Port's a no-go. At this rate, I might be using *you* to get a visa somewhere."

I snort. "Sadly, my South African privileges are fairly limited, Mrs. van der Merwe."

"Not Mrs. van der Merwe." She clucks her tongue against her teeth.

"Technically…"

"Technically, I did not indicate a change of last name on the marriage license. So I am still and forever Mssssss. Moore. We are married on paper only."

Sunlight catches her phone screen, blinding me every time she turns it over in her hand. The somber mood in the car irks me. Today should be a day of celebration, not already burdened with what happens next.

Not ready to declare the festivities over, I crank up the radio and start belting out Icona Pop's "I Love It." I add some arm dancing, eliciting a giggle from Ophie—my goal.

"Come on, ball and chain. Let's go home." I flip my indicator to turn right at the light and get a smack on the arm for my cheek before she closes her eyes with a deep sigh.

"Wake me up when we get there, poopsie. I need a nap."

I don't know if the warmth that spreads through my chest is from the sun shining through my window or from the privilege of getting to see her playful side—not many people have that privilege.

Since the first time I sat beside her in class, Ophie has tested my resolution to turn over a new leaf when I came to the States. My older brother and parents had long given up on me being anything more than the family clown. When I got accepted to the University of Portland's master's program, they didn't have much faith that I would make it to graduation. Not that I could blame them. I'd only graduated from UCT—University of Cape Town, the family alma mater—by the grace of a few professors.

As I pull up at another red light, Ophie closes her eyes, resting her head against the chairback. I allow myself to stare at the way the sun drips across the curve of my wife's cheek for a long moment before I focus back on the road.

I know my parents won't approve of our quickie Vegas wedding, but I am convinced they'll love Ophie. They've chatted with her before over video call. But they'll absolutely lose their minds when they find out what I've done. Worse, they won't be surprised. *If* they find out.

We've already managed eight weeks without anyone suspecting a thing, so I'm starting to think that Ophie's right, and we'll be able to get a quiet divorce in a few months with no one the wiser.

I promised my mum that when I got to America, I wouldn't waste the opportunity I'd been handed and would take my studies seriously. The promise had been fairly easy to keep during orientation. Since we were older than the undergraduate crowd, ours was, disappointingly, not at all like I'd expected from the American TV shows and movies I've seen—not a keg stand in sight. Instead, it had been more like a series of mixers and networking events full of shaking hands and sober discussions of class load and work-study assignments.

Dreadfully dull.

I'd swallowed down the temptation to liven up the gatherings with some great tunes or a hot dog-eating contest. Just.

But when I'd sat next to a dark-haired woman in my second class of the day, something had possessed me. She'd pulled a laptop out of her bag and set it perfectly square on the desk in front of her, then proceeded to set a tiny notebook and three different-colored pens beside it before sitting back in her chair and clasping her hands in her lap.

All of this without a single word or glance at anyone else in the room. As prim and proper as you please. And I'd been overcome with a burning desire to break her—to make her a little messy.

I'd made a comment about her pens. She had pointed out that I had no supplies of any kind ready for the start of the lecture. I'd snagged one of her pens before pointing out that it was the first day of class, and it was unlikely we'd hear anything worth writing down. The shock on her face had egged me on to more and more ridiculous declarations.

We'd kept it up throughout the class, in hushed whispers at first, then scribbling notes back and forth in her little notebook after the professor called us out for being disruptive. If I hadn't caught the hint of a smirk on her face when we got called out, I would have given up at that point. But something told me there was a naughty side to Ms. Ophelia Moore that no one had set free.

She'd balked when I asked for her number, until I explained my hard and fast "no dating while in America" rule. Apparently she had a similar life motto. On the agreement that we were just going to be friends, we'd headed to the nearest coffee shop. The rest, as they say, is history.

"Dude, are those sirens?" I crane my neck to see where the noise is coming from. The movement disturbs Ophie. "Wakey-wakey, liefling."

Beautiful whiskey-brown eyes blink open, and she stares at me with a dazed expression. Her hair sticks up around her face, making her look more like a secretary bird than the starling I usually compare her to in my mind. Wiping her mouth, she looks around in confusion. "What's that noise?"

"I think there's a couple of fire trucks in the parking lot ahead." Checking my rearview mirror, I don't see any more emergency vehicles. But my heart picks up speed as the sirens grow louder the closer we get to my street.

Ophie points to the fire engines clustered near my apartment building. "Oh shit. Philip, is that your place?" She's awake now, her hand trembling as she gestures to the billowing smoke.

"Fuck. That's my kitchen window." I scan the road and the parking lot, the nearest driveway blocked by a police cruiser. "If I just pull in here, can you—"

"I'll take care of it." Her frantic voice cuts me off as she waves her hands, shooing me out of the car. The second I put the car in park, I'm out in a flash, not bothering to close the door as I sprint toward the noise and commotion.

"Sir, you can't go in there." A firefighter steps in my path, blocking me from bounding up the stairs to my home.

"That's my apartment. Is my roommate okay? Was he in there?" I peer over his shoulder, not sure what I'm looking for. Smoke is billowing out of the window in thick plumes, but there's only a trickle coming out of the front door.

"Philip!" Chris calls my name from somewhere behind.

I whirl, catching sight of my roommate. He's leaning against the hood of his car, an emergency blanket draped over his shoulders. "Thank god." Fright still racing through me, I hurry over to him, then clap a hand on his shoulder. "I thought I was going to have to find a new roommate, and you know how hard it is to find a decent one."

Chris laughs at my joke. Now that I know he's okay, my instinct is to make jokes until the panic goes away. To trade the adrenaline of fear with the endorphins of making someone laugh. "So, was it ramen in the coffee maker again? Left a grilled cheese on too long?" The familiar roller-coaster of emotions I've felt my whole life swings from fear to giddiness at the drop of a hat—much to my mum's chagrin.

"Frozen pizza in the oven." He shakes his head, looking sheepish. "I put it in when I got off shift and fell asleep on the couch while I was waiting."

My roommate is a first-year teacher, but since he makes next to nothing, he also has a part-time job bartending at a local restaurant. The man works so much he's hardly home. A perfect roommate, really.

"Is everything okay?" Ophie huffs as she jogs up beside me. "What happened?"

"Chris was just testing the City of Portland's emergency response teams' reaction times." I grin at her, but she doesn't look impressed.

"Only took them six minutes," Chris adds, leaning forward on the hood of the car. His unconcern at the situation only amplifies her consternation. "Hey, how was graduation? Are you two finally going to drop your 'no dating in grad school' nonsense?"

Ophie coughs and turns bright red. His joke catches me off guard too, and I swallow back a surprised curse.

"Didn't I tell you I booked us the honeymoon suite at the Four Seasons?" I laugh off the familiar accusation. No one seems to accept that Ophie and I are just friends. Best friends, sure, but just friends. We drew that line at the beginning of our relationship. A line that had been crystal clear until eight weeks ago.

Chris holds his hands up, the emergency blanket slipping off his shoulders. "Okay, okay, whatever. If you two would just start dating, everyone would leave you alone. You have to admit it's weird how much you two hang out and you're *not* together."

"I hardly think that our dating status is more important than the fact that there is a fire in your apartment." Ophie sticks her hands on her hips and glares at my roommate.

I get caught in the crosshairs as well, but it rolls off my back. She's never really mad at me. Annoyed, for sure, but angry? Never. And I like keeping it that way, so I jump in with my own defense. "We only graduated four hours ago."

"Four hours is plenty long enough to change your relationship status." Chris shakes his head at us before pointing to a man standing beside one of the fire trucks. "Fire chief said it was contained in the kitchen. They have to assess for smoke damage, but nothing outside of the kitchen was burned."

As if summoned by Chris's words, the man makes his way over to the three of us. "Fire Chief Mason. You the other roommate?"

"I am." I hold my hand out to shake his. His eyebrows dart up at my accent, then furrow in thought. He's about to ask me where it's from, guaranteed.

"Are you English?"

And there it is. For as much as Americans like to watch British television, ninety-nine percent of them assume that's where my accent is from. You'd think between Charlize Theron and Leo's decent attempt in *Blood Diamond,* more people would recognize the accent.

"South Africa—Cape Town, specifically. Any word on the damage?" I cut the twenty-questions game short, impatient to know the worst.

The fire chief takes his baseball cap off and runs a hand through his hair before he answers. "The kitchen sustained the bulk of it, but there is smoke damage throughout. Unfortunately, you won't be able to stay in the home for the time being. Do you have somewhere else you can stay?" He tips his chin in Ophie's direction. "Your girlfriend's house?"

He directs the question to Chris, and I have to restrain myself from growling at him. *My* wife takes a hasty step away from Chris and closer to me. "Yeah, I have space." She looks up at me, her brown eyes full of concern. "Maggie's all moved out now, so I have a spare room. Chris, do you have somewhere to stay, or do you want to sleep on my couch?"

"Thanks, but I already texted my boyfriend, so I'm good."

"I won't be able to let you in to get anything until tomorrow at the earliest, just as a safety precaution." Chief Mason glances back at his men still buzzing around the parking lot and front door.

I shrug. "I'm pretty sure she's stolen enough of my hoodies and sweatpants that I'll be fine for a day or two at her house. Do you need us for anything else, or…?"

Once he verifies he has our contact information, he declares us free to go. I'm sure this is going to be a pain to deal with, but not one I can do anything about tonight. With a final wave to Chris, Ophie and I head over to our cars.

"See you at home, Mrs.—"

Ophie's hand slapping across my mouth cuts me off before I can finish teasing her.

"Do. Not." She growls the words, glancing around the empty parking lot.

I wink at her and step back into a small bow. "Ms. Moore. Shall we?" I know she doesn't want anything to change between us, and even though it breaks my heart a little, I'll keep pretending that's true. Starting by not using this unexpected stay at her house to my advantage.

Ophie holds her glare for another moment until she dissolves into giggles. Forcing a laugh, I lean against my car, facing her. "Oph, you know nothing's changed, right? We're still friends. It's just a piece of paper. Insurance in case it takes longer to find a job than anticipated. Fingers crossed, we never have to tell anyone about it."

The tension releases from her shoulders as they sag, and I pull her in for a hug. "Promise?" Her voice is muffled against my chest but still audible. Or maybe it's just that I'm so used to hearing it that I could pick it out of a crowd anywhere.

"Promise." I kiss the top of her head, something I've done often in the past. I've even done it a hundred times in the last eight weeks, and nothing was different. It's the most natural thing in the world and yet somehow, in this moment, with my heart still pounding from the shock of coming home to my place being on fire, entirely new.

I'm still puzzling over the change, unable to pin down exactly what's different, when we pull up at her place and I take the parking spot her sister used to claim. I heard all about Maggie and Kel's roundabout romance last fall from Ophie. She was rooting for them from the start and treated me to long diatribes on the awkwardness of Kel's pursuit of her sister.

"You know you can stay as long as you need, right?" She looks back over her shoulder as she lets us into the condo. It's a small place—just two bedrooms and a single bathroom—but she and her sister have done their best to make it nice. Maggie has a flair for color and decor, and most of it is still here.

The familiar white couch squeaks as Ophie flops onto it, her chunky heels dangling precariously off her feet. "I don't know if I need a nap or a shower."

I pull her shoes off and set them beside mine at the front door before dropping into the easy chair, my legs splayed in front of me. "Nap. Definitely a nap first. At least we never have to write another paper again."

Peering at me from underneath the arm draped over her face, she grimaces. "Don't remind me. I don't want to think about my thesis or the problems with the Oceania ports of call ever again. And I'm working the morning shift tomorrow."

My head thunks back on the edge of the chair as I groan. "I still have ten essays left to grade for Higgs—damn him and his acceptance of late work. Grades are due at midnight tomorrow. Why did I decide to TA for an Economics 101 class?"

Rustling and grunting sound from Ophie's direction before she replies, "Because the US immigration system is confusing as fuck, and the only job your counselor thought you could have with your visa was as a TA."

I lift my head to glare at my best friend. She's rolled over to sprawl facedown on the couch, her dress barely covering her ass as it sticks up in the air because she didn't bother to remove one of the many cushions that decorate it. "Right. That." Normally, I would reach over and smack her bum without a second thought, but now I hesitate.

We both swore that getting married wouldn't change anything between us. But somehow, everything suddenly feels different.

Ophie

I GIVE UP TRYING to shower quietly when I drop my shampoo bottle for the third time in a row. If the clatter didn't wake Philip up the first or second time, then either he can sleep through the noise or he's awake anyway.

My four a.m. alarm felt obnoxiously loud when it woke me up this morning, and I'd turned it off in a hurry, unlike my usual three-snooze-button routine. Of course, this means that I'm twenty-four minutes ahead of schedule, leaving me time for a proper hair wash before heading to my opening shift at the coffee shop.

God, I can't wait to find a real job. I never want to start work at five in the morning again.

Yawning, I finish showering, letting the hot water wash away the remnants of my tossing and turning. I don't know why I was so jumpy all night—I should have slept like the dead after yesterday's drama.

Maybe it was because I fell asleep on the couch while we were watching a movie last night. Yes. That had to have been the problem. It's definitely not because having Philip here feels weird. Or that when the movie finished, I woke up with my back pressed against his chest, his arms wrapped around me, and his soft breath tickling my ear. Philip's always been physically affectionate with me, kissing my head all the time, but we've never cuddled like that before. It was dangerously comfortable.

I haven't exactly avoided him since we came back from Vegas, but I haven't gone out of my way to hang out with him, either—both of us being overwhelmed by the end of grad school made it easy to keep some distance. Ever since the Elvis impersonator officiating our Vegas nuptials told him to give me some sugar, and Philip gave me a quick, sweet peck on the lips, there's been an unsatisfied feeling in the pit of my stomach. A feeling that roared to life last night when he nuzzled his face into the crook of my neck, making the most adorable sleepy noises.

He's spent the night on my couch or in Maggie's room dozens of times before. There's no reason it should have felt different last night.

Except it did.

My hair can't decide if it's straight or wavy, but the one thing it is for sure is thick—drying it is a commitment. A commitment I can't deal with today, so I push all the weirdness from my mind as I braid back my hair for work. Right now, I can't be thinking about the man who's asleep in my spare room.

Towel wrapped around my torso, I open the bathroom door and run straight into a wall of man chest. Echoes of my vows to love him tender and love him sweet sing at the back of my mind while I stare at the muscled pecs in front of my face.

"Good morning to you too." Philip grips my arms, holding me steady as I gape up at him. When I don't move, he slides his hands to cup my elbows, picking me up and moving me to the side. "Gotta use the loo." He drops a kiss on the side of my head and then closes the door in my face.

Stunned, I stand there staring at it for a moment. I'm naked. He was shirtless. Does he really not feel like everything is different now? Also, why am I still thinking about it? He's being perfectly normal. *I'm* the one being weird.

I hurry to my room and force myself to focus on getting dressed and ready for work. By the time I emerge, the bathroom door is wide open, and his is shut. Pausing outside the closed door, I listen but don't hear anything. He must have gone back to bed. Which makes sense since the sun's not even up yet.

It's so overcast that the sky barely changes as I drive to work, adding to my internal grumbling. The end of spring in Portland is either gorgeous or miserable, and there is no in-between. Growing up in Seattle was the same, so you'd think I would be used to it, but every spring, as the gray skies drag into June, I get antsy and irritable about it. I've been dreaming of the sunny skies in Las Vegas and the memory of baking by the poolside to get through these last few weeks of gloom.

My shift is the usual Sunday morning parade—the regular before-church rush, then the more leisurely crowd, with some of my regulars sprinkled in between.

"That guy is hot," one of my coworkers whispers in my ear as I pass her behind the bar.

"Which guy?" I'd been taking out the trash, and there definitely hadn't been anyone I'd describe as "hot" when I'd left the front of the coffee shop.

Sarah tips her chin toward a scrawny white guy with greasy hair and chin fuzz. "The one in the corner who looks like he's waiting for a job interview." He's fiddling with the tie around his neck and drumming his fingers on the table beside his cup.

I raise an eyebrow at my coworker. "Seriously? Raise your standards, Sarah."

"What? He's cute," she objects. "He kind of looks like Pete David-son."

"Yeah—also not cute. I don't understand the appeal at all." I shake my head. "At least go for a guy who looks like he bathes regularly."

My words conjure up an image of Philip showering at my place, and a new and unwelcome zing shoots through my core. This is ridiculous—he shared the hotel suite with Sydney and me in Vegas, and I didn't react like this. I am losing my mind.

But Philip definitely bathes regularly. He always smells delicious.

"Whatever, Ophelia. At least I do something about being interested in a guy." Sarah shakes her head at me as she pulls a carton of almond milk out of the fridge.

"What is that supposed to mean?"

A woman walks through the door, and I move to take her order.

Sarah pours milk into the metal pitcher for steaming and gives me a look. "It means you talk a lot of game about who people should date without ever dating yourself. You and Philip just do that weird thing you all do."

I don't have a chance to respond before the customer starts rattling off her order while Sarah flips on the machine's steamer, drowning out anything else.

I don't date because I don't *want* to date. A fact nobody seems to understand. With how things ended with my college boyfriend, I don't trust myself not to pick another narcissist. And after I nearly didn't finish my undergrad because of him, I vowed never to let a penis derail my plans again.

Besides, I've been too busy with school and work and have plenty of friends. Past me made sure that present me doesn't have the burning desire to have "a man" in my life that everyone seems to assume I do.

I have Philip and a vibrator—what else do I need?

"He's my best friend. It's not weird."

Sarah gives me a look. "Him being your best friend isn't the weird part. It's the fact that you guys act like a couple but claim that A) you're not attracted to each other. Hello, you're both fucking hot, so that's one hundred percent bull. And B)—" She stops to scoop some ice into a cup. "Whenever anyone tries to ask either of you out, you always use the other as an excuse not to."

I don't have a chance to argue before a team of preteen girls in soccer uniforms, plus their families, walk in the door. It's an endless stream of blended drinks and pastries until I clock out for my lunch break at ten.

Snagging a sandwich from the cooler case, I wave to Sarah, then take it and my drink out to my car. The sun has come out, and even though it's still chilly, I want to bask in the warmth of it on my cheeks. As soon as I close the door and crack a window, the weight of being surrounded by people is baked away by the sunshine seeping into my bones.

My older sisters are both natural extroverts—Daisy lives for showing off her perfectly curated life, and Maggie is the living embodiment of a golden retriever. My whole life, I thought there was something wrong with me because I like being alone so much more than they do.

Discovering what an introvert is at the age of seventeen was a true lightbulb moment for me. And I've been constantly surrounded by people for the last few days. I think the only time I've been alone is in the bathroom. And even though Philip has never triggered my need to be left alone before, I'm suddenly so aware of his presence in my house that I can't relax.

I dig my phone out of my pocket and scroll through it while I eat. Recently, my algorithm has taken to showing me a combination of baby cows, food porn, and women who have given up on the male species. I'm not mad about it—especially the baby cows.

A video with helpful tips for writing a dissertation pops up on my feed, and I quickly exit the app. I only have five minutes left of my break, and I refuse to spend any more minutes of my life thinking about my thesis. Or anything else to do with school.

Can't think about school.

Can't think about Philip.

I'm not sure what's left to distract myself with.

I fire off a quick text to my sister, including a picture of a quokka for Kel's daughter Olive. She's been obsessed with them for the last few weeks.

By the time I drag myself up the steps to my house hours later, the countless cups of caffeine I've consumed to keep me on my feet are making me jumpy and sick. I unlock the front door and, for a second, question if this is the right place. Voices echo from the kitchen, and the smell of some kind of meat cooking wafts in on the cool breeze coming from the open patio door.

"Hello?" I hang my purse and coat on the rack, then toe my shoes off and line them up neatly below.

"Hi there!" Philip calls from somewhere in the house. The voices cut off abruptly, and he pokes his head out of the kitchen. "You're hungry, yeah?"

"Starving." My stomach growls as the smell of what he's cooking hits me again. "Do I have time to shower? I was on bathroom cleaning duty right before I left."

"Yup, it'll be ready now now."

I stop in my tracks and give him a look. "Okay, you say that all the time, and I have no idea what 'now now' or 'just now' means. Like, 'right now' or 'in a bit,' or what? It's been driving me crazy for ages."

Philip's cheeks turn pink beneath his scruff. "Um. It means in a little bit. It's a bit vague, to be honest." He shakes his head, then clicks the tongs in his hand. "I'm just cooking some chicken, and I made a salad. Is that alright?"

"Sounds good." I take a few steps down the hall when I can't think of anything else to say. This awkwardness between us is new and unwelcome. He has cooked at my house before. He's being his usual charming and thoughtful self.

I chastise myself through a quick shower, slipping into a pair of sweats and a tank over a clean sports bra. Following my nose, I find Philip in the kitchen, plating up the food.

There's a perfectly sliced chicken breast lying on top of a bed of salad greens, feta cheese, olives, cucumber, and tomato. "This looks delicious. Thank you for cooking." I pop up on my toes to give him a kiss on the cheek, like I've done a thousand times before, and take my plate. "Do you want to watch a movie? Or finish season three of *The Witcher*? I was rewatching *Bridgerton*, but I didn't think you'd be interested."

"I'm game for *Bridgerton* if you want to keep watching it." Philip says it just a little too casually. The moment I press play, I realize why—this is not the same episode I was on the other night. Glancing at the guilty party beside me, I stifle a snort at his pink-tinged cheeks while he carefully avoids making eye contact. I nudge him with my shoulder and settle in to rewatch season two.

I'm hyperaware of his shoulder occasionally bumping mine, and the way his thigh presses against me when he leans forward to set the remote down on the coffee table in front of us. All things that have happened a million times before, but now I have Sarah's words echoing in my head.

I don't use him as an excuse not to date, do I?

I'm only half watching the show as I puzzle it over. Sure, a few guys have asked me out over the last few years, but I wasn't interested in them enough to make the time for a date. I was taking fifteen graduate credit hours, plus writing my thesis and working at the coffee shop, so where was there time for a boyfriend? I've been a graduate for less than forty-eight hours. Surely no one was expecting me to run out and get a boyfriend the moment I crossed that stage? Is it too much to ask for stability in one part of my life while everything else is changing?

Having to start my career, convince my family I'm not moving back to Seattle, and get ready for my new niece or nephew to arrive is enough to deal with, right?

What Philip and I have is perfect. We keep each other company when our friends drag us out, and if I'm ever lonely—which I'm not—I know I can count on him or Cassie to come over or meet up for a drink. All without the pressure of being a girlfriend. No one expects me to do his laundry, cook for him, clean up after him, or take care of him when he's sick.

Reassured, I settle back into the couch and focus on the TV, stuffing my face with the delicious dinner *he* had ready when I came home from work.

"Are you alright?" Philip asks as I set my plate down, empty of every-thing except a stray piece of lettuce.

Every inch of me tenses. Am I being weird? I thought I was acting naturally, but maybe I'm not? I turn my head to look at Philip over my shoulder. "Why?"

"You're very quiet."

"Uh…" I move in slow motion, easing myself an inch away from his warm body. My stomach clenches, my heart races, and I don't know what to do with my body. Worse, now all my arms and legs feel too long.

Last night, we were both so tired after the graduation ceremony and dinner with my family that we'd fallen asleep on the couch. Tonight, I'm tired, but not too tired for my mind to spin in circles, wondering how Philip feels about what happened.

Concern fills his face. "Did you not like it? Or did someone give you a hard time at work?" He reaches out to tuck a stray strand of hair behind my ear, and I hold still. "Oph?"

My heart slows at the touch of his fingers. A giant exhale escapes me, and I lean into his hand for a moment. "Work was fine. I'm just very peopled-out."

Philip pulls his hand away and sits back. "Do you want me to leave? I can go—"

I grab his arm before he can finish standing up from the couch. "No, not you. Just. *Other* people. Yesterday was a lot, you know? I feel like I've been putting off being a real grown-up until graduation. But now we've graduated, and I don't feel any different."

He chuckles, and my heart slows a little more as he sits back down and throws an arm around my shoulder, pulling me close. "It was definitely a lot. And dinner with your whole family. And now I'm invading your space too. My poor little introvert is overwhelmed by people."

A laugh bursts from my lips, and I cuddle in closer, wrapping an arm around his waist and settling my head against his chest. I've done it a thousand times and never thought twice about it. Despite the waves of awkwardness that have been washing over me, this feels right.

Pushing my silly thoughts away, I exhale and melt into my friend, the last of the tension I've been feeling leaving me in a rush.

"Good?"

I nod against his chest. "Much better now."

Philip

MY BROTHER'S FACE KEEPS freezing at the most inopportune times. Bad for him. Good for me, as I take screenshot after screenshot of him looking absolutely terrible.

I don't currently need to blackmail him, but it never hurts to be prepared.

I also know for a fact that Jonathan has a folder of similar screenshots of my face on his phone. His wife told me. It's why, even though it's late and I'm ready for bed, I keep myself from yawning—nothing looks worse than a photo of you mid-yawn.

"…Mum's blood pressure medication."

"Jono, you cut out. What about Mum's medication?"

"The doctor is reducing her dosage. Apparently, leaving Cape Town was good for her heart." Jono laughs at something off-camera. "Hold on, Flip, someone wants to say hello." Everything moves wildly, and the sound of my nephew's little voice hits my speakers. I settle deeper into Ophie's couch, my head tipping back to rest on the back of it while I wait. She's working a closing shift, and I was half waiting up for her, half waiting up for my weekly phone call to my brother.

A moment later, the scene stops, and the screen fills with the cherubic face of my two-year-old nephew. "Unca Pee-Pee? Where you?"

Did I say cherubic? I meant booger-encrusted and suspiciously wet.

Jono roars with laughter, and the screen goes wild again. Henrik's cries of "Unca Pee-Pee, where Unca Pee-Pee?" get progressively louder as the phone is wrestled away from his sticky hand.

Jono's wife, Nicola, comes on screen laughing. "Sorry, sorry, Flip. Davy was trying to teach him to say 'Uncle Flippy,' and things devolved from there. I'm afraid you may be Unca Pee-Pee forever now. They've been saying it everywhere we go for days."

I burst out laughing at the image of my nephews, four and two respectively, chanting "Unca Pee-Pee" over and over in public while my sister-in-law and brother try to shush them. Delightful payback for any embarrassment I might have felt. I wonder how much it would cost to get a shirt printed up?

"Philip?" Nicola says my name again like she's been trying to get my attention.

"Yeah, sorry. Just pondering the feasibility of shipping some 'Unca Pee-Pee' merch to my favorite nephews." If shipping to Australia wasn't so ridiculous, I'd do it, too.

"How's the job hunt going?"

"It's going." It's a constant ticking clock in my mind—I only have six months to find an employer to sponsor me before my student visa expires. Thinking about it makes me itchy, so I push to my feet and pace, needing the movement to settle my mind as I change the subject. "At least the weather's finally turned nice. I was going to lose my mind if there was one more rainy day."

"It's still so strange to me that you graduate in May. Why don't they do it in December like normal people?" Jono takes the phone from her, handing off Henrik in a practiced maneuver.

I sit back down on the couch, one of Maggie's many decorative pillows at my back. "Hemispheres." The switch from Southern to Northern Hemisphere seasons had been odd, but not as difficult for me as the lack of sunshine. "How's work?"

My brother launches into a story about some lady who can't seem to respond to her emails without accidentally hitting "reply all" to the entire company. While he talks, my mind wanders to the job listing he sent me a few days ago. It's a position with his company, looking for an international trade analyst. Specifically, they're looking for someone with experience or schooling from America. If I thought she'd consider it for a second, I'd pass it along to Ophie. It's exactly what she's looking for, except she would never move so far away from her family.

As it stands, if I want to move to Australia to be near *my* family, it's perfect.

But for some reason, I'm reluctant to apply.

I've dreamed of living in the States since I was in secondary school. There was a pretty even split in my classmates between going to the University of Cape Town or trying to get out of South Africa. Some to the States, some to England, Australia, or New Zealand.

My mates and I didn't start the diaspora, but we're following in the footsteps of the family members we've seen thriving while living anywhere but in South Africa.

No one wants to end up trapped there, taking care of aging parents on a sinking ship.

"How's Ophelia?" Nicola pushes Jono's face out of the way to steal my attention.

Panic that they've figured out what we've done flares in my chest for a second, before I push it down. "She's fine. I'm at her place right now, actually." I flash the camera to the room around me.

"Oh?" Nicola gives me a meaningful look. "Have you finally realized that your 'no dating in America' rule is silly?"

I bristle. "It's not silly. If I get a green card, I want it to be through my own merits, not because I tricked some poor girl into marrying me just so I could stay." Nausea bubbles in my stomach—isn't that exactly what I've done to Ophie? I feel sick over lying to my family, but they've never understood my need to earn it myself.

"Trust me, Flip, no girl is going to mind being your ticket to stay in the States." She shakes her head at me. "You're being stubborn."

"No, I'm being ethical." The argument is familiar and safe, but the sick feeling in my stomach doesn't dissipate as I dig my grave deeper with each lie. "I was concentrating on school and establishing my future. It's not fair of me to drag a girl into the uncertainty that is my life when I have no idea where I'm going to end up. And it's a little bit illegal to marry someone just to stay in the country."

She rolls her eyes and hands the phone back to Jono, who takes over the argument. They've been together since they were sixteen and I was fourteen—it's annoying how in love and happy they are. "Well, if you get kicked out of the country, you can always come stay with us. Our guest room is always open, or you could crash with Mum and Dad. They've got a posh blow-up mattress now, and you'd only have to share it with the boys occasionally."

Talking about their homes in Australia always stings. I hate that I've never seen them with my own eyes, that I haven't seen my family since I left for America. The familiar pangs of homesickness grate against my thirst for adventure and leave me feeling raw.

I rub a hand over my chest, pushing away the feeling. "I know. Thanks, Jono." Living with my parents again is a last resort—thinking of the last time still makes my chest tight. I'd been all set to go to school in California when Mum was diagnosed with breast cancer. Even though she'd insisted that I should still go, I'd dropped everything to stay in Cape Town.

In the end, they convinced me to at least start my undergrad in Economics at UCT. By the time I graduated, my mum was in remission, and I was desperate to get out of the country. Jono is not only my brother, he's my best mate, but he and Nicola headed to Sydney just before I graduated. Mum and Dad were hoping to follow, assuming I would also be leaving South Africa.

When Portland offered me a scholarship to do an MBA, I jumped at the chance. Even if the Pacific Northwest wasn't exactly the part of the States I'd intended to move to, getting out of Africa was the goal. Now that they've all moved, there's nothing for me to go back for, even if I wanted to.

Only time will tell if the decision was a good one or not.

But I'll never regret meeting Ophie or my life here in Portland for the last two years, even if the lack of vitamin D is painful.

As if thinking about her summoned her, the front door opens behind me, and she steps inside. "Oh, sorry." Her voice is tired as she slips off her coat and sets her shoes on the rack. "Hi, Jono. Hi, Nicola." She knows it's them—she's joined more than one of our standing phone dates on a Thursday night.

Ophie sets a brown paper bag on the coffee table before squishing beside me on the couch, waving to the faces crowding into my phone screen. I bury my nose in her hair, taking a big sniff of the coffee-and-pastry smell permeating it as I pull her into my side.

"Did he tell you why he's at my house?"

Noise filters into my ears, but I'm distracted by her arms wrapping around my waist and the way she melts against my chest. She and her sister hug the same way—full body, arms wrapped around you, leaning in a little. I fucking love it.

Ophie proceeds to tell them the story of my kitchen fire. Not wanting to think about it again, I hand my phone over to her and head to the kitchen. Their exclamations go from amusement at our graduation shenanigans to horror at the fire and then back to amusement when she wraps it up with Chris's confession.

I hand her a glass of water—she's always thirsty when she comes home from work—and sink back down beside her, dropping my arm over her shoulder so she can't escape the conversation yet.

"How long will the damage take to fix?" my brother asks, then disappears from view—probably to wrangle one of my nephews.

"I got a call from the apartment manager today, actually. He said it's going to take a couple of weeks. The smoke damage is pretty extensive, and some of the windows were damaged by the heat and have to be replaced. And of course they're currently on back order."

We chat a bit longer, but when wailing starts up from somewhere in my brother's vicinity, I end the call. "Bye-o, talk to you next week."

"So, how was the fam?" Ophie doesn't move from her spot resting against my chest as she talks.

I relay the story of my new nickname, loving the way her giggles vibrate against me.

"Oh, since I'm off tomorrow and the weather is supposed to be nice, I was going to head down to Sunshine Cellars to see Maggie and Kel. Do you want to come with me?"

There's a list of jobs I need to apply for, but the prospect of spending an afternoon in the sunshine is irresistible. I'll get to the applications later.

Philip

SUMMER ARRIVED OVERNIGHT. THE thick clouds that had been lingering now gone, replaced with a clear blue sky. I'm sure that in a few weeks, I'll be cursing the oppressive heat, but for today, I'm going to bask in the warmth like a lizard. The constant chill in my bones from the damp weather bakes away as sunshine streams in through the car window.

Ophie turns off to the left rather than following the gravel driveway up to the winery's main parking lot. Instead, we park beside a trio of cottages, next to Maggie's sedan. I climb out of the car, following Ophie to the closest of the three. The flowers at the doorstep look brand new, the pot too clean to have been sitting there long.

"Maggie?" Ophie calls through the door when no one answers her knock. "They must be up at the tasting room."

The sound of raised voices drifts back to us as we stroll up the path to the main building. The cottages sit below and to the east of the tasting room, rows of grape vines extending across the south-facing side of the hill beside them.

As we reach the top of the path leading from the cottages to the main buildings, Kel and another man block our way, arguing in low voices.

"You can't be in the tasting room, Nate." Kel runs his fingers through his dark-blond hair in an agitated way.

"Yeah, well, I don't exactly want to be there, but we don't have another option today, do we?" the dark-haired man—who must be Nate—replies, rolling his eyes. "Maggie is sick, and you have Olive this weekend. My mom needs to take Dad to physical therapy. It'll be fine."

Kel blows out hard, turning his head and catching sight of us. His fingers rub circles on his temples in the same way I've seen my dad do when he's trying to figure out how he wants to lecture me this time. "Hey, Ophie. Okay, fine. You run the tasting room today, but please, for the love of god, don't yell at any customers. And when the Suttons show up, be *nice*."

Nate stalks off without acknowledging our presence, grumbling under his breath. Ophie slips her arm around my waist and squeezes. I squeeze her back before extending my hand out to Kel.

"Hey, guys, good to see you. Everything alright?"

We shake hands, but Kel's eyes keep darting over my shoulder down the path we just walked up.

Ophie steps away from me to give him a hug. "We're good. Just needed to get out of the house and get some sunshine. Is Maggie okay?"

"She wasn't feeling well this morning. Could have been something she had at dinner, or it might just be morning sickness. She was up all night and only fell asleep an hour ago." Kel is clearly distracted, his answers slow and punctuated by pauses as he listens for something. He freezes, then pushes past me. "Sorry, I think I hear Olive. I'll let Maggie know you're up at the tasting room when she wakes up."

We watch him sprint down the path in silence. "Do you want to go check on your sister?" I finally ask when she doesn't move.

She shakes herself, then looks up at me, concern in her brown eyes. "No, I'm sure she's fine—Kel will take care of her. I'll text her in a bit."

Taking her hand, I lead her toward the main building. I've only been here once before, but I remember there being a small door on this side of the building. We step through right as another couple enters through the main door.

They look around, taking in the room. The girl smiles when she sees the floor-to-ceiling windows that look out over the rows of vines while her date peers at the chalkboard that lists all the wines available.

I wander over to a small table nestled against the window, dragging Ophie with me as the couple makes their way over to Nate, who's cleaning wine glasses with a soft white rag. The men tip their chins at each other in the universal man language of acknowledgment before Nate leans against the bar that takes up the short end of the rectangular space.

The wooden bar matches the log-cabin feel of the interior—exposed beams grace the high barn ceilings, matching the color of the real-wood floors. The timber walls are a far cry from the plaster used in the Cape Dutch-style wineries I'm used to from home, but it has a woodsy sort of appeal.

I still think a dark thatched roof against a white wall looks better, but I can imagine that might not be the most practical in a place where the air is constantly wet from November to May.

After hearing Kel's admonishments, I'm curious how Nate acts with customers. I lean forward and drop my voice to ask, "What do you think? Is Nate going to be rude to them?"

Ophie leans in to match me, her hair swinging forward and sending the scent of her floral shampoo cascading toward me. "He won't be rude. He may not own the winery anymore, but he still considers it his legacy. It'll be fine."

I glance back at the long bar right as his mouth pulls down in a frown, impatience written in the twitch of his shoulders as the couple stares at the signage behind him.

"I bet you dinner that he's about to make an ass of himself."

"Loser also has to do the dishes?" Mischief twinkles in her gorgeous brown eyes.

I nod. "Dinner, dishes, *and* dessert."

My mind flashes to the idea of having Ophie for dessert before I push it away. The last thing I want is to say something that might drive the only stable thing in my life away. Just because I've found her attractive since the day we met, and she's technically my wife, doesn't give me the right to fantasize about her like that.

Not when I don't think she feels the same way about me.

"Welcome to Sunshine Cellars, folks. What can I get for you?" Nate says the right words, even if his tone isn't exactly friendly. It reminds me of the boys in my standard five class reciting the poems our teacher insisted we learn—they never could do it with feeling.

"Hi. We've never been here before. What do you recommend?" the woman answers. "Our friends were raving about this place, but I don't remember what wine they had."

Nate gives them a pained smile, and I fight back a snort. We have nothing to drink yet, or I would hide it behind my glass. Instead, Ophie raises an eyebrow at me, her eyes dancing with amusement.

"Would you like to start with a flight, then? Today's flight is..." He looks over his shoulder at the board, silent as he studies it. The couple waits without asking, also reading the board behind him. The guy gives his date a meaningful look as Nate struggles to find the information. "Apologies, I'm usually out in the field, not in the tasting room."

Ophie's amusement turns sympathetic as Nate continues with his wooden speech. "Oh my god, this is painful." She shakes her head and sits back while we watch him. After a moment, she waves her hand in that direction. "You would be really good at that. What was that thing your mom said?" Tipping her head, she scrunches her eyebrows. "Right. You could charm the pants off a priest."

We both laugh at that, drawing the attention of the couple and Nate. Our laughter subsides, and Ophie shrinks in apology when Nate glares at her. I raise an eyebrow in his direction when he makes eye contact, and he quickly looks back at the couple and starts his speech again about the chablis-style chardonnay he's pouring.

He can be an asshole to anyone he wants except Ophelia.

We enjoy the entertainment of Nate struggling to stay friendly as he pours the couple's wine. I've been to wineries where they pour them all out at once, but Nate is pouring them a single glass. I assume he'll bring them each new wine as they finish.

It's a great tactic for increasing customer engagement, and I can see how it would be successful with the right person behind the bar, but the constant need to make small talk with the customers quickly reveals that this is not Nate's forte.

Chatting with customers as I pour wine for them? Sounds like a great gig to me.

Eventually, they take their glasses and wander off to one of the other tables. Ophie's staring out the window, her chin resting in her hand. "You want a glass? Or a flight?" I ask as I push to my feet.

"Hmm? Oh, just a glass, please. Can I have the off-dry riesling?"

"Sure thing." I drop a kiss to the top of her head, her flicker of a smile at the action sparking warmth in my chest.

Seeing the sweat breaking out on Nate's temples, I contemplate taking it easy on him and just ordering our glasses without making him small-talk. But what's the fun in that?

"I saw you two come from the cottages," Nate grunts as I approach, leaning down to tuck the open bottle in his hand beneath the bar. "Did you get lost?"

Any notion that I was going to take the high road disappears with his first sentence.

"We were in the area."

Nate's head snaps up at my words, suspicion written all over his face. The pair of wine glasses he'd pulled out rattle as he sets them down on the counter. "Camping? You were camping on the vineyard? This is private property."

"I didn't say we were camping on the vineyard." This is going to be more fun than I thought. He's so easy to rile up. Internally, my hands are rubbing together in glee.

A deep furrow creases his forehead, and Nate drops his voice low as he leans forward, his pouring forgotten. "Where were you camping?"

"We slept nearby."

This is too easy.

"What the fuck does that mean, nearby? You look a little too clean to be homeless. What are you, fucking hippies?" Nate's face is bright red, and his tone edges louder. "This isn't England. You can't walk through people's property here."

"Not from England, mate." I enunciate a smidge more than usual just to make it harder for him to place my accent. Although I am impressed he knows anything about right-to-roam. If this asshole wants to accuse Ophie and me of being vagrants, I'll let him go ahead and dig his own grave. I don't blame him for not recognizing me, but surely he's met Ophie before?

Nate opens his mouth to answer, but then the tasting room door opens, and four women walk in. Immediately, his shoulders go rigid, his jaw clenches, and his eyes roll so hard I think they might flip backward in his eye sockets. Apparently, what I thought was him worked up was just a warm-up.

"Jackie!" A statuesque brunette barrels through the doors. Hot on her heels is a short and curvy blond with the biggest smile on her face. But it drops as she takes in who's behind the bar top. "Oh. Hello, Nathaniel."

"Great," Nate mutters under his breath, quietly enough that nobody can hear except me.

The women stop in the doorway, deep in discussion. Tearing my eyes away from the drama, I look back over my shoulder at Ophie. She's staring at the scene as well, eyes ping-ponging from Nate to the women.

I turn back as I ask, "Regulars?"

"Just his favorite customers."

I jerk back, sending the tallish young woman who appeared at my side into a fit of giggles. Her long blond hair is curled and hangs over her shoulders, swinging as she moves.

Nate rolls his eyes again. "Hello, Emma. You know I can't serve you."

She rolls her eyes right back and leans an elbow on the bar. Her movement reveals an extraordinarily short woman peering out from behind her, her vivid orange hair a sharp contrast to the timid way she looks around the room.

"I wasn't asking you to serve me, was I? Mom has some stuff in the car she needs help bringing in."

The back-and-forth between them is interesting, albeit frustrating since I still haven't been able to get a glass of wine for myself or Ophie.

Nate grunts. "I'm working the bar today. Maggie is sick, and Kel has Olive. Tell your mom to text him to come help. I can't leave here." He jerks a thumb in my direction, and I bristle.

The young girl, Emma, pauses to look me up and down. She's very pretty, in that fresh-faced, college freshman kind of way. Her head tips to the side, lips pursed. "I know you from somewhere."

The declaration takes me by surprise. "Huh?" I shake my head and back up a few steps. "I think you must have me mistaken for someone else. Lots of brown-haired, chiseled types around here."

She snaps her fingers, pointing at my chest. "That accent. You TA'ed for Econ 101, right? My friend was in that class, and I heard you talking to her once. I remember because I thought your accent was super sexy."

"Emma!"

"That's my girl!"

I'd been so focused on our conversation that I'd missed the other two women coming over to the bar. The blond one, obviously the girl's mother, looks like she can't decide between smacking her daughter or hiding in embarrassment. The tall one, who had not been excited to see Nate, is glowing with pride, reaching across the space between us to high-five Emma.

A hand on my shoulder has me whirling, Ophie's laughing face appearing behind me.

Oh my god, I'm surrounded. The five women are all laughing while Nate and I share a look. I still don't like him—his customer service skills are shit—but there's a moment of universal bro-solidarity between us as they laugh at my expense.

"You win. Also, your cheeks are so red," Ophie whispers in my ear, squeezing my shoulder before coming to stand beside me. I want to pull her into my side and hide my flaming face in the crook of her neck, but I don't dare. Not if this girl knows one of my former students.

That way rumors lie.

But fuck yeah, I won the bet.

"Emma, that was so inappropriate." The shorter woman shakes her head. "I raised you better than that."

Emma and the taller woman burst out in peals of laughter. "No you didn't, Sophie. And even if you did, *I* didn't." The tall woman looks back over her shoulder at the orange-haired one. "Frankie thought it was hilarious too. Didn't you?"

She steps around Emma to squeeze between her and the tall one. "Highly inappropriate, but hilarious." She flips her hand out for a subtle low-five with Emma.

The one called Sophie clears her throat loudly, glaring at the other three, who instantly subside. It's my turn to stifle a chuckle as they fall in line, cowed by the maternal vibes emanating from Sophie.

She waits until they're calm before looking away. My god, she's impressive. "Nate, the guys are all out in the parking lot with stuff for tomorrow. I'll man the bar if you could go give them a hand?"

With a sigh that must come from deep in his soul, Nate rounds the front of the counter. "They are doing a flight and need the rosé next." He points to the couple who have wandered outside and are leaning on the porch railing, oblivious to the commotion going on inside.

He jerks his thumb at me, the scowl back. "They haven't ordered yet. Came through the back door."

I don't know what he's implying by that, but he's gone without another word. Sophie takes his place and beams at us.

I'm about to ask what's going on when Ophie steps in front of me, holding out her hand. "Hi, Sophie. I don't know if you remember me. I'm Maggie's sister, Ophelia."

Understanding crosses Sophie's and the tall woman's faces. "Oh, yes, I remember now. How are you? Do you remember Lauren?" She points to the tall woman, who nods. "That's Frankie, a dear friend who works at Mailbox with my husband, and my hooligan of a daughter, Emma."

Ophie greets everyone, then reaches back to pull me closer. "This is my friend, Philip. We parked down by Maggie and Kel's, but since Maggie is napping, we figured we'd come up here and have a glass while we enjoy the view."

Sophie fusses over us, pouring us each a glass of riesling and insisting it's on the house, while I remind myself that I should not be irritated at being introduced as just a friend. This woman obviously knows Maggie, and I promised Ophie her family would never find out about Vegas.

Sophie pours out glasses for Lauren, Frankie, and herself before pulling a can of sparkling seltzer out of a fridge and handing it to Emma.

"Mom, come on," Emma whines, but Sophie just shakes her head.

"You're not twenty-one until next month."

"But—"

"Gotta follow the rules in public, munchkin," Lauren interrupts before Sophie can speak. She swirls her glass expertly and dips her nose inside the bulb for a long sniff. "Mmm, smells delicious, though. As always."

Ophie sways into me, her shoulders shaking from suppressed giggles. My arm instinctively wraps around her waist, pulling her against me. The second my fingers graze her waist, she stiffens, her giggles dissipating.

I let go and step away, a flash of irritation spiking through me. Thankfully, none of the other women seem to notice the way Ophie reacts to me.

My attention is drawn back to them just as Emma rolls her eyes and hip checks Lauren before grabbing Frankie's hand and pulling her toward the window.

Sophie blows out a long breath before deadpanning, "I can't believe you never wanted kids, Lauren. They're such a joy."

"Yours is enough for both of us." Laughing, she clinks her glass to Sophie's. "Do you think the boys need supervision?"

Sophie tips her head in thought. "If Maggie's not there to do it, then yes. Make sure they don't try to do any of the actual decorating. Especially Alfie."

Lauren salutes her and takes off with a small wave.

"What's happening tomorrow?" Ophie asks, sliding onto the stool in front of me. Instead of taking the other one, I lean my elbows on the back of hers, pushing away my uncharitable feelings and determined to act like I always do. If only I could remember how that was.

"Oh, Nate convinced Teddy to restart the wine club. When he bought Sunshine Cellars, Teddy didn't want people joining it just because of him, so he dropped it. But without the wine club members, we have just enough surplus bottles every year that storage is going to be an issue soon."

Sophie pauses to take a sip from her glass, a soft smile on her lips as she swallows. Leaning back on her stool, Ophie presses her shoulder against my forearm, the movement wafting the scent of her shampoo toward me. I catch myself before my eyes can fully close as I inhale. Do I smell her like that all the time? How have I never noticed it before?

"We all love a good glass of wine, but there's no way we can drink enough to keep up. Kel has done such a good job of taking care of the vines that Greg is producing better and better wine all the time. We have to sell more unless we want to be drowning in bottles." Sophie laughs to herself.

"Maggie mentioned she was doing an event here tomorrow, but I hadn't connected that it was actually for Sunshine." Ophie stretches her neck to one side and then the other, the brief glimpse of her long neck teasing me from where I stand behind her. "I assumed it was another shower of some kind."

For a second, I imagine tasting her skin, feeling the softness of it against my lips. With a sharp breath that borders on a snort, I straighten up, pushing the thought away. As I look up, I catch Sophie watching me, an intrigued look on her face.

Dammit. It's been two years since Ophie and I met, and two years since I've had fantasies about her. But ever since Vegas, my mind has been wandering to all kinds of places it shouldn't, and I can't seem to remember how to act normally around her anymore. I need to get it together.

Sophie clears her throat and takes another sip of her wine. "We reached out to the old members to see if they were still interested in the club. A few dozen were, so we're having a relaunch event tomorrow."

The main doors open, and more customers wander in. Sophie greets them with a smile, exactly the opposite of Nate, and Ophie and I excuse ourselves and move back to our table.

"So." Ophie drawls out the word after taking a generous sip of her wine. "What am I cooking for dinner? And what's for dessert?"

She peers over the edge of her glass, waggling her eyebrows and making me laugh.

"I will eat anything you dish up." We clink glasses before taking another sip. If only she knew how true that was.

Ophie

Philip's rendition of "Wannabe" gives me the giggles every time. It doesn't matter that I've seen it plenty of times over the years of our friendship. At karaoke. Stone-cold sober in the car. Slightly tipsy in his living room. Very tipsy in Cassie and TJ's kitchen.

I don't know if it's the memory of him doing the dance from the music video on the stairs of the school library, or the fact that he does the little knee-jiggle move every time they sing "Zig-a-zig-ah" that makes me giggle the most.

Philip is always making me laugh. It's one of the reasons he's my best friend.

Right now, he's bouncing against the seat and singing loudly as he drives us home from the winery. The windows are down, the early summer breeze whipping through the car and tangling my hair as I sing duet with him.

A Kylie Minogue song comes on next. Apparently, South Africans are very into her, but since it's not a song I know, I let Philip sing along by himself while I gaze, boneless and brainless, out the window at the fields of sheep. My mind is fuzzy and soft with a combination of wine and knowing that Philip has everything under control.

The music volume dips, and Philip drops his hand to my thigh, squeezing to get my attention. "You know, I didn't think I'd be meeting an honest-to-god billionaire when I woke up this morning."

I stare at his hand on my leg, not registering his words for a moment as his heat sears into my skin. Forcing myself not to react to the touch, even though it's taking up the majority of my brain space, I pull my hair back in one hand so I can answer without eating it.

"Maggie talks about Nate and Greg so much that I forget the Suttons actually own it. I've never met Lauren or Frankie before. Or Emma. They're a riot," I add as Philip puts his hand back on the steering wheel. For a fleeting moment, I consider taking it back, before sense wins out.

"Emma is trouble. I shudder at the thought of her and Sydney ever meeting." Philip adds a dramatic full-body shake to emphasize his point, and I giggle.

"She's a spitfire, for sure."

"Okay, Grandma." Philip reaches over to poke my side. "Who says shit like 'spitfire' these days?"

I poke him back. "Like I didn't hear you complaining about your back being sore as we walked out to the car."

This is the kind of banter with my best friend I've been missing. We fire away at each other as the road slips by beneath the wheels.

"I helped move a lot of tables." Philip pulls one hand free of the steering wheel to flex his biceps. Not that it was necessary. I'd been admiring the way his muscles flexed beneath his T-shirt all afternoon.

"Thank you for helping. Maggie deeply appreciated it, even if you really didn't have to." When my sister finally woke up and came up to the tasting room, it was clear that she still wasn't feeling well. I didn't realize how bad her morning sickness had been until today, but despite how she glows with happiness every time she looks at Kel or Olive, it's painfully obvious she's struggling.

"She was in no shape to be moving shit."

"There were four other men there." I'd ended up sitting with Lauren and Sophie while Frankie and Emma scurried around with decor under Maggie's direction. I'd been filled in on which man belonged to which woman and laughed at the stories Lauren had told of their various romantic journeys.

All four men were as different as their significant others, but the contrast of Julian's imposing, tattooed frame beside Frankie's fairy-like body was especially entertaining. I kept waiting for him to pick her up and tuck her under his arm like a football.

"Maybe I just didn't want to look like a lazy do-nothing in front of my wife."

My stomach drops and twists, just like it does every time Philip calls me his wife. "Don't," I warn him with a heavy sigh.

"Don't, what?"

I can hear the teasing in his tone. I know he's not trying to start a fight, but even in the car with just the two of us, I can't help feeling like someone is going to overhear. Nervousness fills my stomach and my lungs seize.

"You're not my husband." I'm met with silence. The combination of anxiety and wine bubbles up in me, bypassing the filter that usually keeps my thoughts contained inside my mind. "I mean, you *are* my husband. But, like, we're not in a relationship. Well, we are, but it's a best-friends relationship. Not a...Not a romantic relationship. We don't do romance. I don't even know if I know *how* to do romance anymore. I like things how they are. Don't say things that remind me things are different—"

"Ophie." Philip cuts off my rambling. "Everything is exactly the same between us. Nothing is different." He reaches out to turn the volume up on the music, and I melt back into the seat to stare out the window.

I definitely had a little too much wine because, for a second, I'm convinced I hear him mutter "unless you want it to be."

Google Maps is not improving my mood. "An hour? I don't remember it being that far." I let my head flop back onto the couch, my phone slipping off my legs onto the seat beside me.

"What's an hour?" Philip sets down the coffee mugs in his hands and sits beside me.

"Remember how I applied to a million and one jobs last week? I just got a request for an interview."

"So why aren't you happy? Because it's an hour away?"

I nod, not bothering to sit up and take the coffee he made for me. "It's at a paper mill in Longview, Washington. I wasn't exactly being picky when I filled out all those applications."

Philip takes a long sip of his coffee before giving me a look. "Desperate times call for desperate measures. At least you won't get deported if you can't find a job right away."

The reminder of how this started cuts through my irritation, turning it back to more familiar anxiety. Now with added "I committed immigration fraud" flavor and a dash of "I enjoy living with Philip so much more than I was expecting," just to be confusing.

"Even if I was working full-time at the coffee shop, which I'm not, it's not enough to keep up with rent on this place for much longer." With a groan, I sit up and take the mug waiting for me on the coffee table. "But it's an hour away, and I just don't want to."

We sip our drinks in silence for a moment, the early morning sun peeking through the blinds bathing his golden skin in light. After two weeks of him being here, I've finally stopped squeaking every time I see him shirtless, but that doesn't mean I don't appreciate that my best friend is attractive as fuck. And somehow manages to stay tan, even in the winter.

"How about I go with you?"

"What?" I cough as the coffee I was in the middle of swallowing almost goes down the wrong tube.

"I'll drive you to the interview."

"You don't have to do that."

"I know I don't. But I want to." Philip leans forward to set his mug down. "Come on, we'll make a day of it. I'll drive so you can get all Zen and shit. I promise to sing all the way there if it helps keep you distracted. And afterward, we can either come straight home or go on a little coast adventure."

He's determined to make this happen now, I can tell by the look on his face. There's a particular set to his jaw and glint in his eye he gets when the word *adventure* comes out. If I try and deny him the chance to come, he'll either pester me until I relent, or he'll hide my keys on the morning of the interview so I'm forced to let him drive me.

Opting for the path that leads to less anxiety and annoyance on my end, I relent. "Fine. You can drive me. And we'll get lunch or something before we come home. I can't go to the coast, I have to work a closing shift that afternoon."

Philip's face relaxes when I agree, the stubborn squint gone from his eyes. "It's a date." He grins and is gone before I can argue over his choice of words.

By Tuesday afternoon, I'm regretting agreeing to let him come as he leans against my doorway, one arm lifted, his hand gripping the top, and one foot crossed over the other. "Your thirst-trap posing has no effect on me." Ignoring him, I put the black blazer in my hand back on the rack as Hozier's latest song starts blaring from behind me.

Turning, a navy-blue pantsuit in my hand, I'm presented with my best friend/husband lip-syncing the words as he rolls his hips against the doorframe. He grins when my cheeks flame up. "You sure?" he interrupts his lip-syncing to ask.

I nod and hold the pantsuit up in front of my body. "Better?"

"One of these days, Ophelia van der Merwe, God is going to smite you down for all your lies." Philip grins and switches to twerking off-beat with the sultry music, making me laugh. "No pantsuits in a paper mill."

"My lies? Excuse me, Mr. van der Merwe, but I am not the one who faked 'stomach issues' to get out of Professor White's pop quiz." I hang the pantsuit back up and pull out a black pencil skirt and wine-colored blazer combo. "And that's Ms. Moore."

"With your white button-down." He nods to the outfit in my hand and pauses the music. After strutting across the room, he takes them from my hands and hangs them up on the hook on the back of my door. "You're going to be great. Now stop fussing and come help me. Then you're going to bed to get a good night's sleep."

Taking me by the hand, Philip drags me out of my room and to the couch, where his laptop is sitting open on the coffee table. "What do you think?"

I settle beside him and pull his laptop closer. Big bubble letters spelling out "Unca Pee-Pee" are splashed across the screen in different color combinations and gradients.

"You were serious? Nicola and Jono are going to kill you."

The grin that splits his face overflows with mischief. "I know. I'm going to get them matching shirts too. This is going to be the best Christmas ever."

I glance out the window at the setting sun, then at the clock in the corner of the screen. It's past nine o'clock and still light outside, but the air is chilly. It may be the middle of June, but the nights are still cool. The AC unit in the living room is quiet—I turned it off when I came home from work and found Philip napping on the couch with goose bumps covering his arms. My apartment is one of the lucky ones with an air-conditioning unit strong enough to keep the whole place bearable even in the worst heat waves, but it works a little too well in these in-between weeks, as Portland decides whether it's ready to dive headfirst into the summer temps.

It's warm in his bedroom, and I make a mental note to turn it on low before we go to bed.

"It must be so weird to have Christmas in the middle of summer," I blurt out, my mind still on the weather as we get into the car the next morning. As the cool air flows through the AC vents, I direct it on my face to stop the beads of nervous sweat gathered on my temples from rolling down my face and ruining my makeup.

"Nah, the weather isn't the weird part. The weird part is when there's still people dressed up as Santa Claus when it's thirty degrees outside—"

I grin because I love listening to him say "thirty." It sounds like "thut-ty," and for some reason, I find that hilarious. Also, he knows I'm about to comment on his Celsius stubbornness.

Philip slaps his hand across my mouth before I can say anything. "—and sending Christmas cards with snow and evergreen trees." We stop at a red light, and he leans in close, his blue eyes filling my field of vision. Even this close, I can tell he's smiling too. "You Americans and your turkey dinner and snow. You have no idea what you're missing. A Christmas braai with boerewors, roast potatoes, and salad is *actually* the perfect holiday feast."

I pull back and eye him. "Roast potatoes with barbecued sausage? What a weird combo."

"No judgment until you try it."

"I have always wanted to try boerewors." My mouth struggles over the unfamiliar word. "Boo-ra-vors? Bore-worst?"

Philip bursts out laughing and pulls away from the light. He keeps laughing as he merges onto the highway toward Longview. "Boo," he starts, waiting until I echo him.

"Boo."

"Re." He rolls his *r* in a way I can't quite copy, but I do my best.

"Vorz."

"Vorz."

"Boo-re-vorz." A brilliant smile tugs at his lips as he says it slowly, and I copy as best I can. "We'll make an Afrikaner of you yet."

We spend the rest of the hour-long drive with Philip attempting to describe various South African foods to me, and I have to admit, several sound delicious. We violently disagree on the correct color of cream soda, though. Cream soda should absolutely never be electric green.

He keeps me distracted and at ease until he pulls into the parking lot of a large warehouse beside the river fifteen minutes before my interview.

"Right-o, Mrs. Hot Stuff. Here we are."

"Mrs. Hot Stuff?" I turn to him, one eyebrow raised.

He shrugs and grins, head tilted to the side. "Just trying it on for size. What do you think?"

"No." I laugh and sink into my seat, fiddling with the ends of my fingers. The nerves Mr. Hot Stuff had been keeping at bay refill my belly as I pick at my nails. A hangnail on my right middle finger catches against my other hand, making me flinch. If I don't take care of it now, I'm going to end up ripping it and bleeding on my white shirt.

Pulling my purse onto my lap, I scavenge through the pockets for my clippers. "'Mrs. Hot Stuff' sounds as if the Hot Stuff is actually you, so it's not a compliment to me. It makes me sound like an accessory to your already established level of hotness."

Which is not a lie, but I would never admit it.

I keep speaking, not looking at Philip while I hunt for the elusive cuticle nippers. "I'd prefer for my nickname to be based solely on my own merit, not my pretend husband's. Besides, I already have one."

"Technically not pretend, liefling," he points out, using the nickname he gave me a few weeks after we met—the one I've never looked up the meaning of because I'm too scared of ruining our friendship to look too deeply into it.

My fingers close over the clippers, and I pull them out to snip the hangnail before it drives me bonkers. Philip is uncharacteristically quiet as I focus on my fingernails. "You okay?" I ask, not looking up.

"Yeah..." He sounds distracted, so I lift my head to see what he's doing. "There are a *lot* of men around here."

I open my mouth to point out the obvious—this is a mill and a shipping yard—when it sinks in what he means. Groups of men, four and five to a pack, are moving around the parking lot and adjacent shipyard. I've never been catcalled by a construction crew, but it feels distinctly as though that might happen the moment I step out of the car.

As we stare at the scene, mouths agape, and I mentally berate myself for picking the tight pencil skirt and not my wide-legged trousers, another car pulls up and parks a few spots away. A short, full-figured woman steps out and scurries toward the door marked *Office*. She's wearing dark jeans and an ill-fitting polo shirt, with a chunky brown cardigan over it. I don't miss the way she clutches her purse to her chest and barely looks around as she moves. A chorus of greetings and whistles surround her, which she only acknowledges with a backward wave and zero eye contact.

"Hmm." Philip echoes my thoughts as the door closes behind her. He picks my left hand up from where it rests on the edge of my purse, his long fingers playing over the ring on my middle finger. The cheap one we bought from a vending machine in Vegas that I've kept on my middle finger since we walked out of the little chapel on the Strip. "Do you want me to walk you to the door?"

I hesitate, my independence warring with fear. I study the clock on the dashboard. Seven minutes until my interview. "I'll be okay. I'm sure they're all just talk. Besides, you'll be able to see me the whole way."

Nerves churn in my stomach as he keeps playing with my ring, twisting it on my finger. "Fine. But—" He slips the ring off and replaces it on my ring finger, an artificial wedding band that somehow calms some of my fear.

"Philip..."

"Just humor me." When he looks up, his mischievous smile is back in place. "Please?"

I huff out a chuckle. "Fine. But only because you asked nicely." Pulling my hand away, I click my purse closed, determination snapping into place. "Wish me luck!"

The second my hand lands on the door handle, Philip pulls me back. I'm not ready for it and fall back, catching myself against the center console. Instead of kissing the side of my head like he always does, his lips land on the edge of my mouth. And since I habitually air kiss whenever he does it, what should have been a perfectly normal, platonic goodbye between friends becomes Philip and I actually kissing.

On the lips.

For longer than a peck.

We separate with a choked gasp, and I immediately scramble out of the car. My lips burn with the memory, but I ignore it and pull my blazer straight before slinging my purse over my shoulder.

As I close the door, the sight of Philip frozen in place, one hand covering his mouth and eyes wide, sears itself into my mind. While he looks as if the world just moved two degrees off its axis, I feel like a buzzing in the depths of my brain has quieted. The fact that what just happened left me feeling calm and settled instead of confused is a puzzle I'll have to sort out later.

Right now, I have an interviewer to impress.

Philip

Ophie's strained smile drops the moment she turns her back on the man shaking her hand. From my vantage point in the car, I can see her pissed-off expression and the way his eyes linger on her backside as she walks away. Both have me a heartbeat away from getting out of this car and punching him in the face.

The only thing that keeps me in my seat as she stomps toward me is her delicate middle finger waving in the air in response to one of the guys loitering around the lot when he shouts something to her.

"Don't ask. Just drive." Ophie drops into the seat, anger vibrating off her as she buckles her seat belt.

"Yes, ma'am." Putting the car in reverse, I turn to look back as I pull out of the spot. My thumb brushes her neck as I grab the back of her headrest to look, and I swear she shivers. But maybe that's just wishful thinking. She's probably trying to shake off whatever happened in there.

I let the silence stretch on while I navigate us out of the parking lot, but as I turn onto the main road away from the port, I can't take it any longer. "What happened?"

Deflating, she closes her eyes and slumps before taking a deep breath and straightening in her seat. "He started the interview by calling me 'little lady,' and it went downhill from there."

"Ek gaan hom aan die plafonwaaier hang en soos biltong laat uit-droog." The insult pours out of me, courtesy of a particular high school biology teacher.

"Um...what? I caught biltong. What does beef jerky have to do with it?"

Ophie's confused question breaks the tension, and I laugh before answering. "It translates to 'I'm going to hang him from the ceiling fan and let him dry out like biltong.'"

Her tinkling laugh fills the car, and the part of me that was worried she was hurt finally relaxes. "That sounds perfect. He'd deserve it. They're not looking for a project manager, they're looking for a maid who will go around cleaning up all their messes while wearing a low-cut blouse and a tight skirt."

Squeezing the steering wheel, I stop myself from growling. "Yeah, I saw him checking out your ass as you walked to the car."

Ophie makes a retching noise. "I should have flipped him off too."

I turn my music back on as we ease onto the highway, keeping an eye on the directions from my GPS. It takes only a few moments for my brilliant best friend to realize we're not going back the way we came.

"Where are we?"

"I made a discovery while you were in your interview. Trust me?"

Please let her say yes, please let her say yes. The idea started as a joke, but the more I think about it, the more I want to check out the landmark I found while poking around Google Maps. I'd been trying to distract myself from obsessing over that accidental kiss, and it led me down a fascinating rabbit hole. Besides, it's obvious that she's in desperate need of the kind of fun only I can get her to enjoy.

Not that kind of fun.

I wish.

"Yesssssss." She draws the word out between her teeth, biting her bottom lip as it fades.

"It's a fun surprise, I promise."

Silence stretches between us for a long moment, and then, to my delight, she takes a deep breath and does a full-body shake. "Sure. Let's do it. Anything to forget that interview ever happened."

"Your wish is my command." I give her a little salute before turning up the volume on the radio, Icona Pop blasting as we drive. By the end of the song, Ophie is singing along with me. Hearing her slightly off-key voice cracking on the high notes settles the last of my worries.

I spent the whole time she was in that interview worried that my impulsive actions had thrown her off her game. That the accidental pressing of her lips to mine had left her as confused as I was.

Sure, I've kissed the top of her head or her forehead a million times. I can't help it, she's just so damn adorable when she's flustered. And even though we shared a sweet, albeit chaste, kiss in Vegas when we tied the knot, the way she'd walked away from the car like she was ready to kick ass and take names, while I was pondering why that kiss had felt both familiar and electric, has been eating away at me.

But I push all those emotions away and focus on driving and singing with my best friend who just had a shitty interview and needs a distraction.

Not Mrs. Hot Stuff is too busy singing along with Sabrina Carpenter to notice the road signs that might give away where I'm taking us. There are surprisingly few signs out, but I suppose the movies came out more than ten years ago, and the hype has died down. The vampire franchise was nowhere on my radar until the marked house popped up in maps. It helps that we binge-watched the movies last weekend while she was feeling rough from her period.

"Um, where the hell are we?" Ophie sits up, looking around as I drive down a tiny residential street. Squarely middle-class craftsman homes line the sides of the road. "There's nothing down here except houses—"

She snaps her mouth shut as I drive between two massive cedars whose branches meet to form a tunnel overhead. There's a small sandwich board in front of the third house on the left. Leaning forward, she braces her hands on the dash to read it. "The Swan house?"

I pull over to the side of the road. "No werewolves or vampires in residence, unfortunately."

"Oh. My. God." Ophie sits staring at the familiar white house, the siding pristine and the yard better kept than those in the surrounding areas. "It's really the house from the *Twilight* movies?"

When I nod, she bursts out laughing. "How the hell did you find this? Daisy is going to be so jealous."

I tell her about my map rabbit hole as we climb out of the car. Leaving her blazer behind, she wanders toward the house, telling me about the short-lived Team Edward vs. Team Jacob feud between her sisters back in high school.

As my wife explores, I'm struck by how beautiful she looks in the summer sunshine, the way the light catches the caramel highlights in her hair and outlines the curve of her hips in that skirt.

I should be focused on my own job hunt, not obsessing over making my best friend happy. If I want to stay here in the States and have Ophie be part of my daily life, I need a job.

The tension melts away as we wander around for a few more minutes, taking photos and giggling, before my grumbling stomach can't be ignored.

"There's a restaurant not far from here. Let's get lunch." I pull a giggling Ophie to the car. We're still laughing as we stumble into the restaurant. The host seating us keeps looking back as she leads us to the far end of the restaurant, and I give her a friendly smile to reassure her that we're not a pair of loonies.

There's a mix of decor on the walls, including some *Twilight* memorabilia. I'm busy studying a faded photograph on the wall beside our booth as I slide in, the hostess forgotten.

Something soft bumps my hip, and I turn to see Ophie has slid in beside me instead of across like she normally would. "Wha—"

"Thanks so much. My *husband* and I are starving. Do you make a good club sandwich? I'm dying for one, haven't had a decent one in ages." She wraps her hands around my upper arm, cuddling in beside me. "What do you think, babe?"

Before I can answer, the host is gone, her ponytail bouncing as she speed walks away from us.

"What was that all about?"

Instead of answering, she releases my arm and slides over, leaving six inches of space between us. Six inches too much.

"Nothing. I've just had my fill of ogling today."

"Ogling?"

Bright pink stains her cheeks, and she dips her head. Her response is half muttered and barely audible. "She was checking out your ass as you slid into the booth."

I turn toward her, my eyebrows raised, waiting for her to make eye contact. It takes a moment, but when she does, she sighs. "I thought she was going to lean over and take a bite out of it."

"So you decided that if anyone was going to take a bite out of my ass, it would be you?"

She twists in her seat, setting her elbow on the table before resting her chin on her hand. The position pushes her lips together, a cross between the infamous duck lips of our youth and a pout that I can't seem to stop staring at. "Technically? Yes." She grins, making me laugh out loud.

With my focus still glued to her lips, I'm dying to know how she feels about that accidental kiss, the words sitting on the tip of my tongue. But everything between us is so easy, so fun and carefree, that I don't want to disturb it.

We've both been so careful to keep our relationship on safe, platonic ground—each of us for our own reasons. But the tension between us ever since Vegas has been simmering and building.

Our lives are in upheaval right now, and I don't want to add to the complication. Who knows where either of us might get a job offer? Ophie's kept her job search to the Pacific Northwest so far so she can be near her family, but I've applied to places all over the country.

Not that I want to leave her.

But I might not have a choice, so I push the curiosity clawing at me to the side and focus on finding out what other companies she's waiting to hear back from. Ophie fills me in on the companies she is most excited about applying to, while I sit entranced as she tells me about them.

The server who comes to take our order looks like he couldn't be more than eighteen. His brown hair sticks out at all angles as if he forgot to brush it, and the wispy scruff on his cheeks isn't thick enough to hide the still-red scars from his last bout with acne. But he's old enough to look Ophie up and down in a way that has me immediately on the defensive.

If he doesn't stop trying to see down her shirt, I'm going to deck him. I don't care that I easily outweigh him. He looks scrappy, so I'm sure he'd be fine once he learned his lesson.

He checks her out every time he passes us, which means that every time I start to get my irritation under control, he goes and triggers it again. By the time we're done eating and getting ready to leave, the pit of my stomach is a churning mass of anger and mediocre BLT.

"I hope everything tasted alright?" he asks Ophie as he drops off the check without acknowledging my presence. "Is there anything else I can get you, ma'am?"

Something in me snaps, and I throw my arm over the back of the bench, my hand dropping casually over her shoulder, effectively blocking his view of her cleavage. "The bacon was a little undercooked, but otherwise fine." I lean forward to make eye contact. "How was your club sandwich, *babe*?"

Ophie twitches under my arm, pushing back toward the bench and forcing me to stop my stare down with the teenage letch. She turns to look at me, one eyebrow raised and a playful smile on her face. "It was good. And my bacon was fine." She looks over her shoulder to smile at the server.

He smiles back, and Ophie gives a little laugh. The annoyance I've been pushing away ever since he first glanced at her chest bubbles over inside me. Instead of joining in like I think she expects, I reach up with my free hand to grip her chin. "You got a little—" I swipe a speck of salt off her lip, and her eyes go wide, caught on mine as she freezes. The server behind her coughs, and in my peripheral, I see him turn away, but I'm trapped by something I can't identify flitting across her face.

Without thinking, I lean forward and kiss her.

Not just a peck either. I crush my lips against hers, using my grip on her chin to pull hers apart so I can capture them with mine. For a second, she's frozen, and then Ophie kisses me back with the tiniest little sigh escaping her. One of her hands rests against my thigh as she leans in, and I tense beneath her touch.

In one smooth movement, she pulls back and slides out of the booth. By the time I've gathered my two remaining brain cells together, she's halfway across the restaurant, headed toward the door.

Well, fuck me.

I think I might be in love with my best friend.

Ophie

THE YEARS, MONTHS, WEEKS, days, hours, and minutes that Philip has wormed his way into being the most important person in my life shift by an infinitesimally life-altering breath as he kisses me.

I've never thought about what his lips would feel like, but as soon as their softness registers in my mind, it's as if that's exactly what I expected them to be. Same with the way he lightly sucks my bottom lip, his fingers firm on my chin. I never anticipated knowing what it feels like to truly kiss Philip, but now that I have, it feels inevitable.

I bolt from the restaurant as soon as I come up for air, because if I don't, I might do it again.

My heart races as I pace outside the restaurant. I know Philip. He couldn't have meant anything by it. I'm overreacting. Right? Yes. Yeah. Definitely. The buzzing in my fingers is just from surprise. The look in his eyes before he kissed me—determined and sure—wasn't life-changing.

Nope. Definitely not.

"Ophie?"

Philip is out of breath as he steps outside. The sun catches on his hair, highlighting the curls that he never bothers to tame. His sunglasses are already on, hiding his eyes, but not the worried wrinkle on his forehead. He pauses, glancing back over his shoulder before giving a small shake of his head and closing the space between us.

Throwing his arm over my shoulder, he squeezes me into his side as if nothing unusual had just happened. "I'm sorry."

Confusion replaces the tingling in my spine, and I crane my head to look up at him, but he keeps staring straight ahead as we walk back to where we parked. "Sorry?"

"I took it too far." He shrugs as we pause by the side of his car. I slip out from under his arm and turn to face my friend. His cheeks are the slightest bit pink, and he still won't look at me as he pulls his keys out of his pocket and clicks the button to unlock the doors. "That pipsqueak kept trying to look down your shirt."

Halfway to reaching for the door, I straighten and turn around to face him. "The server?"

Oh.

My confusion settles down as I realize that Philip was doing exactly what I'd done—what we've done dozens of times for each other when on the receiving end of unwanted attention from the opposite sex.

"Well, I figured since you already loudly claimed me as your husband, I could return the favor." He finally looks at me over the top of his sunglasses as he finishes his sentence. His eyes are clear, the playful glint I'm used to back in place.

Why does it irk me that he seems so unaffected?

That he's acting like everything is back to normal. I should be relieved.

With a sharp nod, I turn away and slide into the passenger seat. Like the gentleman he is, he closes the door for me, and I take the few seconds I'm alone to tuck my feelings away. I'll deal with them later.

If my fingers would just stop buzzing.

"You know your phone is ringing?" Philip jerks his chin at my hand as he buckles his seat belt.

"What?" I look down. Sure enough, the reason my fingers have been buzzing nonstop since I left the restaurant is not because my best friend just kissed the pants off me, but because my sister is calling. A swipe to look at my recent calls shows that not only has Maggie been calling me every few minutes, but so has Sydney.

"Shit." I accept the call, nearly dropping my phone in my hurry. "Maggie? What's wrong? Are you okay? Is the baby okay?"

"Finally!" Maggie's breathless voice greets me. "Are you working this afternoon?"

"Um. Hi. And yes. Philip and I are just heading home now so I can get ready. Why?"

"Oh! Is Philip there? Can you put me on speakerphone?"

I'm going to lose my shit if she doesn't explain herself soon, not that I should be surprised. If I could barrel through life the way she has, I'm pretty sure I wouldn't have the emergency Xanax prescription in my bedside table.

I tap the button to put her on speakerphone. "Yes, Maggie, Philip is here."

"Hi, Maggie. Everything alright?" Philip glances at the phone as he throws an arm around the back of my seat, backing the car up and turning with that smooth one-handed motion that is unreasonably hot.

"Hi, Philip. I seem to recall Ophie saying you have some experience with wine. Is that right?"

He raises an eyebrow in my direction, but I just shrug. I have no idea what Maggie wants. "If you mean did I spend a few summers as a teenager working at our family friend's vineyard in Stellenbosch, then the answer is yes. But I wouldn't say I have much experience beyond my own drinking of it."

"Honestly, it's not a big deal. You're so friendly, you're the better option even if you don't know anything." Maggie mutters something inaudible before laughing. "Sorry, Kel thinks I should explain the problem first." Again, her voice goes muffled, like her hand is over the speaker.

Mimicking her, I cover mine and look at Philip. "I have no idea what's happening."

He shrugs and grins. "Does anyone?"

"Right. So, long story short, we have no one to run the tasting room at Sunshine this afternoon. Kel has to take Olive to a birthday party, and I have a meeting with a potential client at three, so neither of us can do it. The Suttons are in Canada, and Theo said he'd rather close than have Nate run the room again—he scares off customers."

"What about Greg or Jackie?"

"They left for their cruise last week." Maggie sighs.

"What cruise?"

"Greg surprised Jackie with one of those around-the-world cruises. They're gone for the next three and a half months. Listen, if you can't do it, that's okay." The stress in her tone is obvious, even though her words contradict it. I can just picture her fingers pinching the bridge of her nose like she does when she's in planning mode.

"So, you need someone to come work the tasting room today? I volunteer as tribute, m'lady." Philip flashes me a grin as he eases us onto the highway. "I can be there in about an hour and a half, is that alright?"

Maggie squeals, and I shove the phone away from our faces to avoid hearing loss. "That's wonderful. Thank you so much, Philip! I can man the fort until two, so as long as you can get here by then."

I tune them out as they iron out logistics. Philip will be perfect—he's charming, chatty, and I've never known a person who could bullshit their way through a conversation with more ease. I think it's the accent. Americans are always bamboozled by a British-sounding accent.

We pass the drive home in quiet, occasionally singing along to a song or pointing out sheep, cows, or other animals.

Honestly, does livestock even exist if you don't point and name them as you drive by?

Philip stays quiet as we go inside, dropping an absent-minded kiss to the top of my head on his way back out minutes after we arrive. At the threshold, he turns to watch me as I load our breakfast dishes into the dishwasher.

"I'll see you tonight, yeah?"

I look up from sorting silverware into the basket. He's halfway out the house, a concerned wrinkle between his eyebrows as he stares at me.

"Of course. I'll be home after close."

He nods before slipping out the door, closing it behind him with a soft *click*. I finish cleaning up the kitchen before changing into my work uniform and leaving for the coffee shop.

Midweek afternoons in the summer, when it's finally hot and slightly humid, mean I stay busy behind the bar making iced and blended drinks. The whir of the blender is so constant, I only notice its absence when we have a lull.

Last summer, we had a short stint offering milkshakes and the usual coffee menu, but the owner nixed that option after three different baristas strained their wrists scooping the ice cream. This summer, he added smoothies, which are better for our wrists but hell on the eardrums.

"Ophelia?" Sarah leans in close. "Are you okay?"

"Yeah?" I pause what I'm doing and turn to my coworker. None of my other coworkers know Philip, and I am in desperate need of a distraction. Sarah hates to cook and goes on as many dates as possible so she doesn't have to eat alone. She always has crazy stories, so I was excited to see that we were on shift together today. "Why?"

"You've been mixing that lemonade concentrate for a while." She gives me a meaningful look, and I drop the stirrer in my hand onto the counter.

"Just tired." I shove the pitcher of thoroughly mixed lemonade into the fridge and grab a cup to start working on the next drink.

"Tired? Or distracted?" She bumps my hip with hers, takes the cup from me, and jerks her chin toward the pile of blender pitchers that needs washing.

Grabbing the top one, I rinse and stack. "Okay, maybe a little distracted. But it's no big deal." If I say it out loud, maybe I'll start to believe it.

Sarah finishes making the drink, while I rinse equipment as a lull in customers settles in. I'm drying and putting away a stack of clean mugs when she steps beside me. "Sure you don't want to talk about it? Might be nice to have a neutral party weigh in."

"Are you a neutral party?"

"Well, the closest you've got, baby girl." Sarah laughs just like my mom—she would love her. "You look like you need to get it off your chest. And I promise not to tell."

Maybe I should confide in her. She's not wrong. I am dying to talk to someone, but I know that any of my friends, or Maggie, would stop listening once I said Philip kissed me, and I'd never get a sensible word from them. But how much do I share with her? Do I tell her *everything*?

"So...do you remember how I went to Vegas for Spring Break?" I blurt out the words before I can second-guess the wisdom of confessing my crimes.

"Of course I do, since they brought stupid Jeff in to cover for you." We both shudder at the mention of our old teammate and his penchant for drinking expired milk. "Did you and Cassie get in a fight or something?"

"No. Her sister was an ass, but everyone got along okay. Maybe too well." I pause and grab a towel to wipe down the counter behind me, but Sarah pokes my arm and takes it from me. "Philip and I may have gotten along a little too well." I mumble the words as I grab another cloth for myself.

Sarah whirls to face me. "You and Philip? You finally got together?"

Red-hot flames lick my cheeks. I shouldn't have said anything. Dammit, does everyone think Philip and I should be dating? "No, we didn't hook up in Vegas. Never mind. Forget I said anything."

She snatches the cloth from me with surprising strength. "Ophelia, you can't start telling me that and not finish the story. What happened in Vegas? Or was it after?"

I reach for the trash can to empty the overflowing bag, but she slaps my hands away. "Uh-uh. You're not leaving until you tell me what's going on. I can tell you need someone to talk to. It's written all over your face."

I shake my head, embarrassment closing my throat. She must be able to tell I can't talk because she gently sets the trash aside and pulls me to lean against the counter beside her. We watch the customers in the store for a moment in silence before she squeezes my arm.

"Come on, tell me what's going on. I promise not to say anything until you get it all out." She mimes zipping her lips. "I'm a vault."

"You promise?"

"I promise. You know I live vicariously through you. Besides, who am I going to tell, my cat?"

That gets a laugh out of me. Sarah may be barely old enough to drink, but she's an old lady at heart, and her cat is her baby. My parents are both only children, so I've never had cousins, but I like to imagine that Sarah and I could be.

"Fine. But you can't tell anyone except Momo. And no getting excited." I point my finger at her face until she nods with a grin. "Right. Um, Philip and I kind of got married in Vegas."

Her eyes go wide at my words, and I can see her physically fighting not to say something, so I pause and wait for her to absorb my news. After the longest minute, she swallows and shakes her head. When I still say nothing, she circles her hand in a "continue" kind of motion.

"The reasons aren't important—" I'm not going to make her an accessory to immigration fraud. "—but obviously, we haven't told anyone. Nor are we planning to. Everything was fine, totally normal, until graduation two weeks ago."

I fill her in on Philip's apartment fire, running into him in the bathroom, and the accidental kiss in the car.

"You what? Fell into his face and kissed him?" Sarah finally interrupts me. The more I've said, the more ridiculous the whole story sounds. Who falls face-first into their friend and kisses them? In real life, not in a movie?

"Technically, *he* fell on *my* face. But yes. That's not even the weirdest part." I turn my back to the coffee shop and lean on the counter, burying my face in my hands. "We went and got lunch afterward, and the hostess was checking out his ass. I think I must have temporarily lost my mind, because something in me snapped, and I got all possessive and made a big deal about him being my husband."

The word is just as unfamiliar on my tongue now as it was this morning. And the same jealousy that had eaten at my stomach as I watched the hostess's eyes drop to Philip's, admittedly very fine, ass burns at my chest. The way she'd bitten her bottom lip had been the final straw. That ass and that smile are mine, not some teenage wannabe influencer's.

"So, you got jealous? You obviously care about each other—that's clear to anyone who sees you two together. Why do you think it affected you so much this morning?"

I shrug. "I don't know what's different today. But it feels like everything is spilling over. How did I not know how strongly I felt about Philip until now? And I haven't even told you the worst part."

"There's more?"

A customer walks in before I can elaborate. I hurry to the register to take their order, Sarah jumping into action behind me to make their drink. When we're done dealing with their order, another customer comes in, and we're kept busy crafting drinks and pulling pastries. By the time we hit another lull, Sarah has eyed me so many times I'm afraid her face is going to get stuck like that.

"What could possibly be worse?" she asks as soon as the counter clears of people.

"Worse may not have been the right choice of words..." I stall, trying to sort out how to tell her. "So, I was wearing my white button-down shirt, and you know I'm not exactly flat on top."

"Yes, yes. You are definitely not a member of the Itty Bitty Titty Committee. No offense, but you're just my ex-boyfriend's type. He had a thing for brunettes with D-cups and hips." Sarah waves away my sputtering with a wink. "Come on, spit it out already."

Self-conscious, I cross my arms over my chest and push my tits down. "I guess the server kept looking down my shirt. I didn't notice at first, but it was pretty obvious by the time we were done. It annoyed Philip the same way I got annoyed by the host, and he—" I pause to gather my courage before confessing what has had me tied in knots all evening.

"So help me, if you don't finish that sentence, I will make you clean the bathroom every shift for the next month." Sarah glares at me.

"He kissed me. Like, really kissed me. Kissed me like I was his real wife, not just on paper," I blurt out, my face already burning up.

"And?"

I'm tempted to throw a cloth over my head to avoid her judgement. Instead, I settle for looking around the shop, a glance at the clock telling me we only have another thirty minutes until closing. "And I liked it."

"Good god, that's it? You're telling me a smart girl like you is twisted up in knots because your best friend, who is objectively attractive, kissed you like he meant it and you liked it?" Sarah swats at my backside. "Go clean tables and think about why you're ridiculous."

I do as I'm told, not that I need the time to know I'm being silly. I don't need my master's to admit that Philip and I have been straddling the fence between dating and friendship for years. The carefully constructed line we'd established at the start of our friendship is built from the knowledge that he's only here temporarily and my determination not to repeat the mistakes of my undergraduate years.

But then I'd caught him scrolling through his phone in Vegas, looking defeated by yet another rejection. I could blame it on the shots I'd been downing with Cassie all afternoon. Or knowing that we were close enough to graduation to feel a little risky. But *The Proposal* had flashed through my mind, and I'd Sandra Bullocked my way into snagging my own Ryan Reynolds.

Kind of. If the roles were reversed. And Sandra Bullock's character wasn't a total asshole. And obviously no trip to Alaska. The parallels are very nebulous, but I really like thinking of Philip as Ryan Reynolds. If you squint and ignore the hair, he could be.

Finishing up my thesis and studying for finals let me pretend I hadn't married Philip on a whim. Or that a secret part of me was disappointed that the moment our Elvis impersonator had pronounced us husband and wife, Philip hadn't confessed that he'd been in love with me from the start.

Ever since graduation, my excuse not to think about our relationship has vanished. And I've done nothing but think about the fact that I *want* Philip to want me.

Thankfully, Sarah lets the topic go as we close the coffee shop and clean up. After locking everything up, we walk out to our cars, parked beside each other in the back corner of the lot. She hasn't said anything else about my situation, but she's had a thoughtful look on her face that means I'm in for a parting shot of advice before she heads home.

"Can I make a suggestion? As your friend?"

There it is. "Sure." I brace myself, knowing I'm not going to like it, because Sarah always gives me uncomfortably good advice. She may be younger than me, but she's lived a lot of life.

"When you get home, try kissing him again. Like you mean it."

"Sarah! That is not helpful. We're just friends. Besides…" I let my real fear slip out. "What if he doesn't want it? Doesn't want me. That might make everything worse."

It has occurred to me that if I wanted to hook up with Philip, now would be the perfect time. He's staying with me, we're both at loose ends, and when things go south, he'll likely be leaving Portland. I won't have to live with the disappointment of yet another failed relationship.

Sarah unlocks her car and tosses her purse into the passenger seat. "Or, you find out that he does. Better to know than live in limbo."

"Is it? At least there's no risk of losing my best friend if I don't."

"But what if you lose the love of your life because you were too scared to try?"

Philip

FLIPPING THE SHOWER TO cold didn't help. Neither did working the tasting room at Sunshine Cellars all afternoon. It almost managed to distract me from the breathy sound Ophie made when I kissed her. Almost.

But as my dear old dad always says—almost only counts in horseshoes and hand grenades.

Which is a really fucking dark saying for my dad, who I don't think has ever had a dark thought in his life. Which is probably why I remember it.

When I arrived, Maggie gave me a quick tutorial on the payment system and an even quicker rundown on the wine list before she left for her meeting. I'd muddled along okay, only having to text Nate for help with the payment system once, and then waited for Kel to come back to shut everything down for me.

And the whole time I'd been chatting with customers, I couldn't stop thinking about how Ophie's lips had felt against mine. And how much I wanted to do it again.

Was she thinking about me while she was at work, the same way I was thinking about her?

To distract myself, I'd picked up dinner and settled in for a binge-watch of Miyazaki movies. Nothing like my childhood favorites to keep me from thinking very unchildlike thoughts. When that didn't hold my attention, I pulled my laptop out and started scrolling through job opportunities and submitting my next round of applications.

My plan was only partially successful, so I threw myself into the shower in an attempt to cool myself off enough to go to bed. The end-of-June heat wave creeping up on us isn't helping the situation.

As the cold water runs over my body, I focus on the goose bumps it raises along my skin. My cock, who's been twitching for attention every time I think about Ophie, stubbornly refuses to settle down. There's so much heat built up inside me that I'm surprised the water doesn't hiss and steam.

I shut the shower off with a curse, then dry myself before wrapping the towel around my hips while I brush my teeth.

"Philip?" Ophie's voice rings through the tiny space.

I make an incomprehensible noise, my mouth full of toothpaste and spit.

"What was that?" She pops up in the doorway of the bathroom, surprising me. I whirl to face her with a gasp. Or it tries to be a gasp, but mostly toothpaste goes down my throat and up my nose. A cough explodes out of me at the same time as a sneeze.

My whole body twitches and jerks as I cough and splutter. Finally getting some air into my lungs, I manage to turn and spit what's left in my mouth into the sink. Ophie is making all kinds of noises beside me, but my eyes are watering so hard, I can't see her clearly.

"Oh god, I'm sorry," I pant out.

"Move over." She pushes me away from the sink, and I stumble a few steps. The water turns on as I sit on the edge of the tub to catch my breath and survey the damage.

Ophie is leaning over the sink, splashing water on her face like a Noxzema commercial. Streaks of my toothpaste spit drip down the doorway, and a splotch is visible on her shoulder nearest me.

"Oh god, Ophie, I'm so sorry." Now that my breathing is back to normal, I push to my feet.

She straightens, eyes closed and water dripping off her chin. "Towel?"

I snag hers from the rack and hand it to her. She scrubs her face dry while I stand there like an idiot, hands flapping uselessly. If dancing from foot to foot wouldn't dislodge my towel, I'd be doing that too.

"Are you okay? I'm so sorry. You startled me, and I inhaled—"

With a final scrub, the face I've been obsessing over all afternoon emerges from the towel, baby hairs sticking up in all directions and makeup smeared. She takes one look at me and starts belly laughing. "I'm fine, I'm fine," she gasps out between chuckles. "I was not expecting to walk into a face full of toothpaste when I came home, but I'm fine."

"Are you sure? I got toothpaste all over you." I pluck at her black polo shirt. "Can I wash this for you? I feel terrible."

All the movement has loosed the towel around my hips, and before I can move, it drops to the floor.

Ophie and I freeze.

Oh god, please don't let her look. If she looks, I don't know if my half-hard cock will go limp in embarrassment or stand to attention. And I don't know which would be worse. "Fuck," I croak out, before snatching the towel from her limp fingers and using it to cover myself. "Christ, Ophie. I should go before I…" I don't know how to finish my sentence, so I trail off. She's still frozen, her eyes wide and hands still up, as if she hasn't moved since I grabbed the towel.

As a strained silence builds between us, her eyes drop to where I'm pressing her towel against my junk. "I...I should..." I stammer out the words, but she doesn't move aside to let me past her. Instead, she looks up to meet my eyes and bites her bottom lip, making my cock go hard against my fist.

I can barely breathe. What is going through her mind? I just spat in her face, then flashed her. Why is she looking at me like I'm a puzzle she's trying to solve?

"Philip...can I?" Her words are barely audible. But her next words are louder, surer. "Fuck it."

Then she grabs my face and kisses me.

Ophelia kisses me like she means business. Her lips capture mine, her hands cupping my cheeks and holding me still. As if there's any part of me that wants to move away and break this spell. If anything, I'm afraid to even think too hard in case it spooks her and puts a stop to whatever is happening right now. Her tongue swipes out to lick across my lips, sending sparks down my spine, and a moan escapes me.

She pulls back, and for a second, we just stare at each other. My lips burn from touching hers, the imprint of her fingertips on my face seared into my skin as my heart races.

All my reasons for not doing this a thousand times before vanish. All I know is that kissing Ophie feels so good, I could do it a million more times and it still wouldn't be enough. I need more.

I step into her, about to grab her waist, when I remember the towel clutched in my hands. Instead, I press my lips to hers with a frustrated groan, and she melts against me, the centimeters between us sparking with electricity.

At least I don't have to worry about what my breath smells like.

Ophie parts her mouth, and I pull her bottom lip between mine, tugging for a moment before I slide my tongue along the soft skin. With a moan, she opens and meets my tongue with her own.

I don't know how long we stand there in the bathroom kissing. It could be thirty seconds, it could be an hour. Time stops, and everything in the world settles perfectly into place as Ophie's breath mingles with mine.

Her hands haven't strayed from my face, her delicate fingers tickling the back of my neck. Again, I need to pull her closer, but the towel in my hands stops me.

Eventually, Ophie pulls back, taking a step away from me with a soft sigh. Her cheeks are flushed, her lips a little swollen. Beautiful.

Her eyes flutter open until she's looking at me. Strands of her hair are sticking up all over, and there's a giant wet patch on the front of her shirt mingling with the other bits of coffee and cream from work.

A beat later, we both burst out laughing.

"I...I should shower," Ophie stammers, still giggling. "And you should probably put pants on."

"Pants?" The command hits me like a bucket of cold water. Christ almighty, what are we doing? "Right. Yes. Pants would be good." I trip over my own feet getting past her, heat crawling up the back of my neck. As I'm clearing the doorway, there's a tug on the towel in my hand.

"I need that."

I whirl to face Ophie as she pulls hard on the other end, snatching it from my grasp.

The last thing I see before the door closes is her laughing face.

I skedaddle my naked ass to my bedroom, my cock standing at attention and bobbing through the air. The gym shorts I hastily pull on don't do much to contain it, but since I'm never leaving the safety of this room again, I suppose that doesn't matter.

For fuck's sake, what is wrong with me?

The sound of the shower kicking on doesn't help, because now I'm imagining Ophie in there, soap running down her body. With a groan, I throw myself face-first on the bed, squishing my wayward dick beneath me. The ruffled throw pillows Maggie left behind serve as perfect covers for my head so I can't hear the shower.

The two of us have spent our whole friendship keeping a careful distance between us, even though I can't resist kissing her head because, *damn*, does she smell good. And in less than twelve hours, we've crossed the fine line keeping our relationship contained not once, not twice, but multiple times. The line is so blurred it might as well be an invitation, but fuck me if I can figure out what it's an invitation for.

Are we just blowing off steam? Giving in to curiosity? Or does she want more? Do I want more?

God, I want more.

"Can I come in?"

Rolling onto my back reveals Ophie standing in my doorway, as if my confused thoughts summoned her. Now she's the one wrapped in a towel, her hair piled on her head in a messy bun. Her face is clean and fresh, but stray drops of water linger on her shoulders and chest.

I can't tear my eyes away from a lone drop snaking its way down her collarbone and between her breasts.

"Philip?"

I kip up, landing on my feet. "Are you sure that's a good idea?" I ask as I cross the room, drawn toward her like a moth to a flame.

"Is it a bad idea?" There she goes, biting her bottom lip again, peeking up at me through her lashes.

I stop in front of her, my heart pounding in my chest. I don't know if I can say no to her. I've *never* been able to say no to Ophie—not really, anyway. But this version of my best friend feels a little like a stranger, and I can't tell if that makes this better or worse.

She reaches out and starts tracing circles on my stomach, her touch featherlight but completely new and utterly engrossing. My wife, who until five minutes ago I could have sworn I knew inside out, is proving there are still sides to her I've never dared to learn about.

I let her continue for the space of a few deep breaths before I catch her hand with mine. "Ophie, what are you doing?"

She twists her hand and threads her fingers through mine. "Would you believe me if I said I was trying to be brave?" She lifts her chin to stare at me with a stubborn expression I've seen a thousand times, daring me to deny her. As if I could.

"Brave? Or reckless?"

"Both?" She takes a half step closer, our hands trapped between us.

My thumb grazes the edge of her towel. The temptation to flick it open flares through me, but I tamp it down. The need to taste her again, to discover the last few secrets she's kept from me—what she tastes like and how she sounds when she comes—burns in me, but I grit my teeth and force myself to take a step backward.

"Are you sure you won't regret this?" Each time I take a step back to give myself space to think, Ophie follows.

"I'll regret not doing this."

The back of my knees hits the edge of my bed, and I sit down with a surprised *thump.* Mrs. Full of Surprises moves closer, stepping between my knees. Her bare legs are still damp, her skin warm and smooth against mine.

Silent, I surrender to temptation, touching my fingers to her thighs, tracing the shape of them, the backs of my hands brushing the bottom of her towel. I keep my eyes glued to the blue fabric. The curve of her ass is temptingly close, but I'm too afraid of shattering the moment to go any nearer.

"Philip?" Ophie breathes my name as she shifts. Her knees bend and she slides a finger beneath my chin, forcing me to look up at her. "I know what I'm doing."

I swallow hard but don't stop touching her thighs, my hands sliding high enough to hover beneath the swell of her ass. "Why?"

"Why do I know what I'm doing?" Confusion shines in her gaze as she tips her head to the side, one eyebrow lifting.

"Why now? Why me?" I gently cup her ass with both hands and groan.

"Because you're my best friend. My favorite person. And if we don't do this now, what happens when you leave? I'll just always wonder what could have been?" She's so close, her whispered words tickle my lips. "Haven't you ever wondered?"

"Every day since I met you." I squeeze her cheeks and tug her forward. Our chests are nearly touching as Ophie's lips hover just beyond my reach. "You're sure?"

"You're starting to give me a complex, Philip." Straightening, she moves to step backward, but I have a firm grip on her backside and don't let her. She leans back, fists on her hips, and stares me down. "What's the worst that could happen?"

"We ruin our friendship?" I state the obvious while fighting to keep my eyes on her face and not staring at the round swell of her breasts right below my line of sight.

"Do you really think we can go back to how things were after today? With everyone we know constantly asking us if we're dating? Always fighting to prove that we're just friends? Don't you want to just give in? Aren't you as tired as I am of toeing the line?"

The exhaustion in her voice is clear as she speaks. Her face drops for a second, and I can see clearly how tired she is. Before I can say or do anything about it, she lifts one leg and drapes it over mine, her knee coming to rest on the bed beside my hip.

"If you tell me to leave, I will," she says, stepping over my other leg and kneeling on the bed, straddling me. My hands slide to her hips as the heat of her pussy settles over my cock. Silently, he begs me to do something. Anything. Just stop torturing him like this.

My hands tighten on her hips, and I take a deep breath, trying to slow my racing heart. "I don't want you to leave."

Her hands slide up my arms to drape over my shoulders, one hand twirling the hair at the back of my neck. "Do you want me to stay?"

"Yes."

Then her lips are back on mine, where they belong. With a groan, I slide my hands up her spine, dislodging her towel. It falls to the floor, leaving her bare in front of me, but I'm too caught up in the hunger in her eyes to look. Instead, I glide my hands over her torso, feeling every inch of her body. Every inch that had been off-limits to me for the past two years is suddenly mine to explore.

The smooth skin of her back.

The dip of her waist.

The swell of her hips that melts into her strong thighs, gripping me between them.

Her soft belly as I slide my hands toward her breasts.

All the while, I'm kissing her—our lips and tongues a frantic tangle. Her teeth nip at my lips as her fingers weave into my hair, pulling at the curls and sending goose bumps down my spine.

My thumbs brush the underside of her tits, and her chest vibrates with a moan. She bites my bottom lip, and it's my turn to groan as she sucks away the sting.

"Touch me. Like you mean it." Ophie doesn't whisper, doesn't ask. She commands—and I'm only too willing to obey.

I take one of her breasts in my hand and squeeze, massaging it in the palm of my hand as my finger and thumb pinch her rosy nipple. A gasp tears from her throat, her hips rocking against mine. Bending down, I take her other breast in my mouth, flicking the already tight bud with my tongue.

"Yes. More."

I risk a glance up to see she's thrown her head back, her arms behind to support it as she rolls her body. It's magnificent. I go back to what I was doing, sucking and flicking with my tongue, occasionally switching to the other breast. One hand keeps busy with a tit, the other splayed across her back to keep her from falling.

"Hmm, that's nice. Keep going." Ophie is vocal with her encouragement in between her humming and heavy breaths. "Oh fuck, that's good, Philip."

She abruptly stops making noise, her hips stilling. I release the nipple in my mouth with a small *pop* and straighten. A splash of bright pink colors her cheeks, her hands clasped over her mouth.

"What?" I ask, an icy chill running down my spine. "Do you want me to stop? We can stop, it's o—"

Before I can finish my sentence, she's switched her hands to cover my mouth, cutting me off. Now that I can see her face, her eyes are full of mischief, and she's grinning crookedly.

"I can't say your name while we do this." And then she bursts out laughing.

I grip the nape of her neck and flip us over so she's on her back beneath me. "You can't say my name? But you don't want to stop?" I can't help giving a little roll with my hips against hers.

She giggles, stopping herself by biting both lips. "It's just..." Her voice drops to a barely audible whisper. "Not sexy."

I drop my head to her shoulder with a huff. "You can call me anything you want as long as you're okay and not about to run crying from the room."

"Okay, but I can't call you Phil. That's even worse."

The bed jostles as I roll off her to lie on my back, staring at the ceiling. Ophie rolls onto her side, pressing against me, her fingertips tracing patterns on my chest.

"I hate being called Phil." My words are aimed at the ceiling, but as I finish, I move my head to look at her in time to catch her making a face. We lie like that for a long moment, the silence building until I turn to face her. She starts stroking up and down my side. It tickles, but I force myself to hold still.

"What does your family call you?" she asks absently, her face still scrunched in thought.

I laugh. "A) I don't want to talk about my family while we're both naked. And B) if you don't think you can scream 'Philip' while I make you come, you're going to be even more disappointed. Their nickname is worse."

"But what is it?"

"You really need to know right now? While my dick is inches away from your pussy, you need to know my childhood nickname?"

Ophie's eyes widen at my choice of words, but then she bites her bottom lip again. She continues touching me in silence, her fingers brushing dangerously close to my cock before she meets my eyes again. "I do."

I close my eyes and sigh. God, I hope she still wants to have sex after she hears this. "Flippy."

"Flippy?" Her shoulders vibrate with suppressed giggles.

"I told you it was bad." The giggles erupt in a peal of laughter, which somehow does nothing to dampen my hard-on. "Can't you just call me babe? Or handsome."

Ophie scrunches her nose. Her hands had stopped while she was laughing, but now they go back to stroking along my torso. "Well, now you've put too much pressure on me, I can't think of anything."

"Then how about I keep your mouth too busy for it to matter?"

Ophie

ALL THE DISCUSSION OF Philip's nickname has me more and more self-conscious of the fact that I'm naked. With Philip. And my nipples are still wet from his mouth.

I'm a heartbeat away from running from the room, when he declares he's going to keep my mouth too busy to talk. Between the dirty words and his possessive grip on my hip, I freeze.

"Come here, liefling."

With those three words, he pulls me on top of him, the hand that was on my hip sliding to scoop me up and over so I'm straddling his hips, his other hand gripping the back of my neck, bending me over until his lips capture mine.

My awkwardness dissolves as our tongues collide once more. The questions and uncertainties of what happens now disappear, leaving behind the perfect way his lips move against mine. The feel of Philip's hands caressing my back and my tits dragging along his chest. The hard length of his cock pressing through the thin fabric of his basketball shorts.

"Ophie...Ophelia," he murmurs against my mouth between kisses. "Are you sure?"

Instead of answering, I rock my hips, sliding my clit against his length with a groan. I close my eyes and lose myself in the sensation. It's been over two years since anyone has touched me, apart from myself. The pleasure of it is almost overwhelming. Somewhere in the back of my mind, I know I should say something, reassure Philip that I'm not just using him.

But the words are stuck behind the wave of sensation that's building up inside me, and all I can do is gasp out breaths between his hungry kisses and keep the rhythm of my hips as friction sparks between us.

With my eyes still closed, I don't have to see what he's thinking—I know his face so well, he won't be able to hide anything from me, and I don't want to know.

"Ophie." Philip spears his fingers into my hair, pulling at the scrunchie holding it up, and pinpricks of pain dance over my scalp. They don't make me stop. Instead, the pain sends goose bumps down my spine, and I move a little faster, pressing down a little harder against the outline of his dick.

"Open your eyes, Ophie," he whispers as he breaks away from my lips, kissing down my jaw and throat.

I screw my eyes shut, not wanting to look and break the bubble of denial where we can do this and still walk away as if everything is the same. His hands guide my head to the side, giving him access to bite down on my shoulder, sending another wave of goose bumps across my skin.

Philip keeps talking, saying my name, calling me liefling, but I only answer with gasping breaths and moans, too scared to wake myself from this trance.

Pushing up from my elbows, hands braced on either side of his head, I use the leverage to change the angle of my hips, putting a little extra pressure on my clit at the bottom of each movement, an orgasm building just beyond the tips of my toes.

The next thing I know, I'm on my back, and my eyes fly open in shock. Philip holds himself above me with one arm, his other hand holding my chin so I can't turn my head. Can't escape the look on his face.

His eyes are locked on mine, intense and dilated.

His eyebrows are furrowed, like when he's hurt.

A muscle flickers in his jaw from his gritted teeth as he growls out a single word, breaking through my selfish bubble. "Wife."

He punctuates his statement with one hard roll of his hips against mine, shattering me into a thousand pieces.

Philip's face has transformed from hurt to smug as I come back to myself, and I wonder if I imagined it in the first place. "So that's the name that got your attention, huh? And here I thought you were going to smack me for using it."

"I still might." I lift one hand off the bed, moving it toward his arm in slow motion. He watches it with an intense stare, quirking one eyebrow at me when I stop inches from his shoulder.

"You won't."

"How do you know?"

"Because I know you, Ophelia van der Merwe-Moore." He's still nestled between my legs, and I can feel every hard inch of him against my aching center. If that orgasm was a warm-up, a sample of what he could make me feel if we go through with this, I'm in trouble.

Philip leans down and kisses me, his teeth pulling gently on my bottom lip. The not-quite-pain brings me back to focus on our conversation. "I thought you said you were being brave? If you want to be brave, be here. Be in the moment with me." He kisses me again, deeply, his tongue swirling against mine, reminding me how right it feels. "Don't pretend you haven't thought about this a thousand times before."

It's my turn to raise an eyebrow at him. "I haven't."

"Bullshit." He grins to take the sting out of his accusation. "I have," he admits, his grin turning soft.

The pieces of me that had gone all soft and gooey post-orgasm flinch. "Don't ruin this. Don't change everything on me now. I don't want to lose my friend."

The idea that this has all been a ploy to eventually win me over is an unwelcome intruder, but I push it away. *I* started this. *I* came into his room. Philip was going to let it go, not pursue anything. He's the one wanting reassurance from me, not the other way around.

"You won't."

"Promise?" I hate how unsure I sound, but I need to know.

Philip sighs and rolls off me, reaching down to adjust himself as we both stare at the ceiling again. "I promise. But if this is as far as this goes, I need you to walk out of this room right now."

He shifts on the bed, propping himself up to face me, his head resting on his fist as he stares hungrily down at my naked body. It takes all my self-control not to pull the blanket over myself, but I suck in a breath, put on my metaphorical big-girl panties, and leave myself bare.

The bedding rustles as I roll onto my side, mimicking his pose, and stare back. We look at each other in silence. Philip's eyes trace over my skin, burning a path along my body.

Finally, I break the quiet. "And if I stay?"

"Then I'm going to find out exactly how you taste when you come on my tongue. And then what your lips feel like wrapped around my cock, before I finally find out what your pussy feels like. And I will still be your best friend after."

We can do this. Have sex and still be friends. This doesn't change how there's a good chance we'll end up far apart by the time we get jobs. And it doesn't change the fact that once his green card is secure, we'll be getting a divorce.

It's just sex.

So I pull him on top of me, our legs tangling as I press my lips to his. I lose myself in his taste, the rough scruff on his chin, and the feel of his fingers sliding up my arm. Weaving his fingers through mine, Philip holds my arm above my head while he commands my mouth. His other arm slides beneath my shoulder, his fingers wrapping over it from behind.

Holding me still, he breaks away from my lips to trail kisses down my jaw and neck, occasionally nipping at the skin. He keeps kissing back and forth across my collarbone, dipping lower and lower with each pass until he's grazing the upper curve of my breasts.

"Tease," I mutter, stretching up to kiss the tips of his fingers. When he doesn't respond by taking my aching nipples in his mouth like I want, I bend my elbow, bringing his hand to my mouth. Sucking his thumb between my lips makes him pause.

"Oh god, Ophie," Philip groans against my tender skin.

"Do what you did before." I arch up, pressing my breasts toward his face. "It felt so good."

His lips hover close enough that his breath tickles the tight buds screaming for him. "Like this?"

"With your tongue. Like you did before." I pull his thumb back into my mouth and suck hard, circling the tip with my tongue as if I was sucking his cock. I release it with a *pop* when Philip groans. "Like that."

"Okay, new rule. No more teasing." Philip accentuates his words by finally taking my breast in his mouth, his tongue circling and flicking at the tip.

I can't help the noise I make as relief floods through me. Our bodies start moving in rhythm again while he gives my tits the attention they need.

When he releases my breasts from his mouth and starts kissing his way down my body, I catch my breath enough to verbally spar again. "You started it."

"Did not."

"Did too."

"Nope. That was all you, wife."

"Was n—"

Philip cuts me off by sliding his tongue long and slow through my core.

"You win," I gasp out as he licks and sucks, his tongue circling my clit.

"I know." He hums against me. "You taste divine."

Closing my eyes once more, I lose myself to the sensations he heaps on me. His shoulders pressing against the backs of my legs, the tickle of his hair against my inner thighs. One of his strong hands gripping my hip and pulling me closer to his eager mouth. The alternating rough and soft of his scruff and lips on my sensitive skin. All of this would be enough to ground me in the moment, but coloring it all is the thought that this feels so fucking right.

Like this is how it should have been all along.

I push all that aside and focus on the tension building in my spine. Philip keeps going, his tongue spearing into me as his thumb presses against my clit. I'm so close I could scream, but it comes out more like a grunting beg. "More, oh god, I'm so close."

His thumb is replaced by his lips and he sucks my clit between his teeth, while at the same time, his other hand reaches up to pinch my nipple, hard. The surprise knocks me over the edge, and I orgasm again with a guttural cry.

The bed dips as he crawls up beside me, his warm breath tracing a path up my belly, but my eyes are too unfocused to see. Reaching out, I pull him close, my hands roaming over his torso while I catch my breath. I run my nails lightly down his side, giving in to my need to touch him. Goose bumps break out over his skin before I skim over his hip, and I smile, knowing I did that. Hooking my thumb in the waistband of his shorts, I push them down as far as I can.

"Last chance to walk away." Philip slides off the bed to stand beside it, his eyes locked on mine, hesitating.

"If you ask me if I'm sure one more time, I'm going to get a complex, Philip." I raise an eyebrow at him. "Strip."

"I just don't want you to regret it."

It's the same thing he said before, but there's something different in his tone now. A sincerity that curls uncomfortably in my stomach. I push it away and focus on the ache between my legs.

"I regret a lot of things in life, but I won't regret this," I reassure him, scooting forward until my feet land on the floor. I push his unresisting hands away from his shorts and slide them down his legs. His cock is so eager to be free of the fabric, it nearly hits me in the eye as I bend forward to take him in my mouth. We've come this far; I might as well be all in.

"Oh god," Philip moans when I slip to my knees in front of him. His hands rest on top of my head as I take him all the way in, my nose pressing against his belly. "Dit voel so goed."

I release his cock and pull back. "What?"

"That feels so good." With a delicate touch, he traces the side of my face. "Your mouth, Ophelia. It's like heaven."

That's all the encouragement I need. It's my turn to explore his body. I slide my lips and tongue along his shaft. It's thick, but not too long, and fits perfectly in my mouth. I take him all the way to the back of my throat, before tightening my lips and pulling back.

I keep it up, my mouth working as Philip's breath comes shorter and his fingers dig into my hair, encouraging me to move at a certain pace. Groaning my name, he fists my hair and holds me still, then takes a step back. "I won't get to find out what your pussy feels like if you keep that up."

Releasing his grip on my hair, he pulls me to my feet, before picking me up and tossing me on the bed. Then he crawls over me until I'm caged in his arms, kissing me long and slow. I hook my leg over his ass, letting his hard length settle deeper between my thighs. The kissing leads us in a rhythm that travels down to our hips. With each thrust, Philip skims nearer and nearer.

"Fuck." Suddenly, he pulls back, his body freezing. "Ophie, I don't have a condom."

I let out a half-laugh, half-scream choking noise. "I have an IUD. And I haven't been with anyone in two years. I'm good."

"I've kept my negative test streak going since I got here. Hasn't been quite two years, but close. Are you—"

"If you ask me if I'm sure one more time, I'm walking out that door." I cut him off, starting to roll out from under him.

Philip pins my arms above my head in one swift movement. "Thank fuck." Then he slides home inside me, stealing any more words away by sealing his lips to mine.

Philip

IN MY WILDEST DREAMS, I would not have expected Nate Ridgefield to be the person offering me a job.

Granted, it's not a real job.

And it won't solve my immigration problem. But it's better than sitting around waiting for Ophelia to come home so I can strip her naked the second she walks through the door while the student loans I've been living on slowly dwindle away.

Turns out academic scholarships only cover so much of your living expenses.

Nate: *It's just until my folks get back from their cruise. You can even stay in their cottage if you don't want to do the commute every day.*

"Is he that desperate? Or did Maggie have something to do with it?" No one answers, which is good since I'm alone at my apartment and packing up my shit.

The landlord called yesterday to inform me he would refund my last month's rent if I was willing to break my lease a month early so he can finish the renovations without me waiting around. Chris and his boyfriend decided to make their new living arrangement permanent, which leaves me with an apartment I can't live in and no roommate.

I can't believe the universe sent Nate, of all people, to rescue me.

I could keep staying with Ophie, but it's starting to feel a little dangerous how much I want to stay.

Especially after last night.

I can still taste her on my lips when I close my eyes. Feel her hot skin under my fingertips. My cock gets hard every time I think about how good it felt to sink into her. To forget about everything else and just be in the moment with her.

Shaking myself, I shove my phone back in my pocket and grab another stack of books. I slide them into the box, packing around them with a collection of bits and bobs off my desk, and let Nate's offer simmer in my mind.

Three months working in the tasting room at Sunshine Cellars for room and board isn't exactly what I want to put on my resume. But it's better than nothing, and now that I've graduated, my job as a TA is finished.

I pack up more of my shit as I weigh the pros and cons of spending the next few months working at Sunshine. By the time I tape up the last box, it's clear that the only real downside is that I will have to deal with Nate on the regular.

The asshole really is a pill.

Although, if I'm there, then he can stay outside in the field or the cellar where he belongs. Besides, I like Kel, and it would be nice to see him and Maggie more.

Me: *Alright, man. How about we try it out for a couple weeks and see how it goes?*

I don't bother to unpack my car when I get to Ophie's since I'll just have to load it all back up soon. Nate asked me to come out to the winery on Monday so he can give me a rundown on everything I need to know.

"Honey, I'm home," I call out as I let myself in the front door.

Any hope I had that there might be a repeat of last night's fun is dashed by the voice that answers me.

"Hi, shnookums."

Sydney and Maggie are sitting side by side on the couch, feet up on the coffee table. Sydney has a wine glass in her hand and is drowning in a pair of oversized sweats and a giant hoodie that definitely looks stolen from the pile of clothes I left here.

Maggie's hands are folded around the mason jar glass of water resting on her stomach. Her tight tank top and leggings outline her growing baby bump.

"Hello, ladies. To what do we owe the pleasure?" I glance around, but Ophie is nowhere in sight. Maybe she is in the bathroom? I crane my neck to see if she's in the kitchen, but it's empty. "Where's Ophie?"

"She and Kel went to pick up food." Sydney takes a long sip from her wine glass. "We ordered Indian."

I sink into the blue velvet chair next to the couch, sliding down until I can prop my feet up beside the two women's. "Like I said, to what do we owe the pleasure?"

Maggie snorts, the water in her glass sloshing dangerously. "We? What's we? I thought you would be back in your apartment already?"

Sydney sits up straight, eyes on me. "Your apartment? What happened?"

I explain about the fire and how I've been staying here while it was being repaired. Sydney sips her wine while she listens, eyebrows pulled together in concentration.

"Did you talk to Nate?" Maggie asks when I pause. The sound of a car door slamming shut and voices outside have me on my feet and opening the front door.

"He texted me earlier," I tell Maggie over my shoulder as Kel steps through the door with two large plastic bags of food.

Maggie doesn't move but lifts her face to Kel. He pauses to drop a kiss on her cheek when he walks past her. "Are you going to do it?" she asks as Ophie steps inside, gripping a paper bag in one hand and two bottles of Sunshine Cellars wine in the other.

"Going to do what?" Ophie's eyes bounce from me to her sister to me, wide and anxious.

I take the wine bottles from her, and she immediately starts to worry at her nails. "Nate asked me to help out at Sunshine while Jackie and Greg are gone." I hesitate but figure it's better to get it over with. "He also offered to let me stay in their cottage so I don't have to commute."

"Oh. Are you going to do it?" She follows me to the kitchen, echoing Maggie's question.

I stick one bottle in the fridge, sifting through the drawer for the bottle opener to uncork the other. "I said I would give it a try."

Maggie claps her hands from the couch, Kel looking on from the dining table, his face soft. "This is perfect. Oh my goodness, Philip, this is going to be such a help."

Sydney snorts into her empty wine glass. "Let me guess, the great Nate is driving people away with his shitty customer service skills? Did Theo kick him out of the tasting room, or did he actually admit he needs help without Kel or his parents there?"

So, no love lost between Sydney and Nate. She never said a word about him in Vegas, but I wasn't exactly paying attention to her.

"I assume Kel knows more than anyone else. Nate didn't say much, just that he needed help, and everyone said I was 'perfect' the other day."

I finish uncorking the bottle and fill the three glasses Ophie pulled from the cupboard. Sydney slides off the couch to bring her and Maggie's glasses over, setting them beside the others for me to refill.

"Did he growl when he said it?" Sydney rolls her eyes as she waits for me to fill her glass.

"Give it a rest, Syd." Kel slips behind me to pull the water jug from the fridge. "We all know you two can't stand each other. Please don't discourage Philip from taking one for the team."

For half a second, I bristle that he's making himself so at home here, before reminding myself that Maggie lived here until only a couple of months ago, and he must have come over often. I shake it off, then decide it's time for me to lighten the mood and change the subject.

"Hey man, how's the culinary program treating you? Make anything good so far?" I ask, handing him one of the wine glasses. The women bustle around us, Ophie pulling out plates and silverware while Sydney takes Maggie more water.

"The commute from Sunshine is a bitch, but so far it's great."

"The focaccia he brought home the other day was amazing. Although I hate that you have to leave so early," Maggie calls out from the couch.

He grabs two plates, piling food on them both as he talks. "Bread is pretty new for me. I haven't gotten it down exactly how I want, but Olive is loving helping me 'study.'"

"Between him and the baby, I'm going to be big as a house soon." Maggie hums as she takes the plate from Kel, inhaling the steam rising off her curry and rice.

Ophie squeezes beside me, an empty plate in her hand. "Did you get everything packed? I'm sorry I couldn't come help you."

I squeeze her waist as I take the plate she offers. "It was fine, yeah. I didn't mind doing it myself. Besides, one of us has to be the breadwinner." I whisper the last part in her ear, grateful for a chance to feel her warm skin near my lips. Which, of course, makes me think of last night. And there goes my cock, testing the strength of my zipper.

Ophie glares while she scoops rice onto her plate before handing me the serving spoon. "Hush. Not with everyone here."

Still leaning close, I whisper against her neck. "Why is everyone here anyway? I was hoping to get a repeat performance."

"They were here when I got home from work—"

"What are you two whispering about over here? Is there tea? I want the tea." Sydney worms her way between us, her butt jostling dangerously close to my half-hard junk. She's so close, I can smell the alcohol on her breath.

"Nothing." Ophie straightens, conspicuously ignoring me while she scoops curry and a samosa onto her plate. "Sydney, would you grab me a piece of the naan?"

She rips a chunk of the flatbread off, bits of garlic flying into the air and landing on the counter, the bread glistening with melted butter. Instead of handing it to Ophie, she holds it near her mouth. "This naan?"

"Hand it over." Ophie rolls her eyes, hand outstretched. I'm not going to lie, watching my wife scold a grown woman is hotter than I expected. Of course, that could just be because I suddenly can't stop thinking about how much I want to kiss her again.

The Adams/Moore clan descending on us was not in my plan for the evening.

"Speaking of the commute..." Maggie pipes up from the couch. Kel looks up from his spot beside her on the couch, not making eye contact. Maggie glances at him, then lightly slaps his arm. "Don't be ridiculous. My name is still on the lease."

Ophie backs out of the kitchen, abandoning me to Sydney. "What's up?"

"Well, I was thinking, if you don't mind, Ophie...Since the drive out here from Sunshine is not exactly fun, maybe on the weeks Olive is at her mom's, Kel and I might stay here? Just until we find somewhere of our own closer."

"You guys want to stay here. Together?" Ophie repeats, eyes darting my way.

"Well, as beautiful as it is, we don't really want to keep living out at Sunshine since Kel isn't working there anymore. And he starts class so early—he likes to get there by seven thirty—and I have client meetings. It would be nice not to have to get up *quite* so early sometimes." Maggie cuts herself off when she shovels a huge bite of curry into her mouth, peering hopefully over the edge of the plate.

"Uh. Sure?" Ophie takes a seat at the small four-seat table, pulling out the chair beside her with a meaningful glance in my direction. "Like you said, your name is still on the lease. And apparently, Philip is going to go stay at Sunshine, so feel free." She shrugs before turning her attention to her plate of food.

I shove my samosa in my mouth, chewing as I move to sit beside her. Leaning close as I sit, I bump her knee with mine. "You could always come stay out at the winery with me."

"What was that?" Maggie's mouth is full of rice, muffling her words.

"Nothing," I say before Ophie can. "Just that we seem to be playing musical houses. Maybe we can get a discount on a moving van."

Maggie takes over the conversation, teaching me more than I ever wanted to know about pregnancy. I thought it was bad when Nicola was pregnant, but at least she didn't share her gastrointestinal distress stories while eating curry, of all things.

Any chance I had of getting Ophie back into my bed again fizzles away with each story Maggie tells. Sydney keeps refilling our glasses, making it hard to keep track of how much I've had to drink. My head is buzzy and delightfully unfocused by the time Kel slaps his hands on his thighs and pushes to his feet.

"We should go, Sprinkles. I have class tomorrow. Plus, I promised to help Nate fix the tractor once I get home." A grimace contorts his face as he pulls Maggie to her feet. "Don't suppose you're handy with equipment, are you?"

"Sorry, if I can't fix it with a wink and a smile, I'm no good to you, man." I tip my almost-empty glass in his direction. "You good to drive?"

"Yeah, I only had the one glass," he calls over his shoulder. "Maggie drove, anyway."

I glance at the three empty bottles on the kitchen counter. He only had one glass?

"Designated driver for the next six months. Take advantage while you can." Maggie laughs, slinging her purse over her shoulder. She stops to hug Ophie, then Sydney, before joining Kel at the door. "See you tomorrow, roomie," she adds as they leave.

"Did she mean me or you?" Ophie asks, gathering up the dishes on the coffee table. When I move to help, she pushes me back onto the couch and shakes her head.

"Does it matter?" Sydney mutters, her head flopped on the back of the easy chair she's commandeered. "Fucking Nate."

"Why do you hate him so much?" I probably wouldn't have asked her if I wasn't buzzed, but the question pops out before I stop to think about whether or not I should be asking it. Ophie rinses dishes in the sink, the clatter of cutlery and glasses drowning out my conversation with Sydney.

She humphs, lazily swirling the half inch of wine left in her glass, her arm dangling over the side of the chair. For the first time tonight, I'm not trying to watch Ophie in my peripheral vision and finally take a good look at Sydney.

Her hair is pulled up in a tangle on her head, and I can't tell if the black smudges under her eyes are makeup or not. But either way, she looks a little rough.

She rolls her eyes and drains the last of her wine. "Because he's an asshole."

"No arguing there. But you seem to hate him a little extra."

"Do I need a reason?" She turns her glare on me. Her eyes have that slightly unfocused look of someone who's been drinking heavily. Mine probably match, if I'm honest.

I shrug. "I guess not. It just seems personal."

"It is."

I wait for her to keep talking, but she doesn't. Just closes her eyes and sinks back into the chair.

I'm still trying to wrap my head around everything that's happened in the last twenty-four hours. Between Ophie and me. Accepting Nate's offer of temporary employment. Maggie and Kel basically moving back into this place.

"Philip?"

I swivel to face the kitchen behind me. Ophie has a collection of glasses on the counter in front of her. "Can you help me?" She points to the glasses, then the open cupboard door behind her.

With a last look at Sydney, who appears to be asleep, I pad into the kitchen. "Do you know what her deal is?" I ask as I put away glasses while she dries more clean dishes.

"Nope. Maggie says Nate basically abandoned the family when he went to France, especially after his dad sold Sunshine to the Suttons. Everyone was upset, but it does feel like Sydney has an extra grudge. For a while, Kel was the only person who would talk to him. No one else in the family would even say his name."

I reach out to take the glass she just finished drying, my fingers sliding over hers. A shiver runs down my spine, and my cock, who finally got the message to settle down, wakes up. We freeze, my eyes glued to her hand beneath mine. "Ophie..."

"I know, we need to talk, but not right now." Her focus darts to Sydney, asleep in the chair, before she peers back up at me. "Don't look at me like that. We can't."

She's wearing her usual post-work sweatpants and tank combo, which shouldn't be hot but is anyway. The way her breasts push against the ribbed fabric, her sports bra squishing them together and creating a valley that calls to me. The baggy material sitting loose against her curvy hips—I want to slide my hands under it and feel her skin again. Prove that last night wasn't a dream.

"Can't what?" I tease, not wanting to drop it, but not wanting to push it and have her walk away.

"Can't do...you know. What we did last night. Not if Sydney is here."

"Are you saying that if Sydney *wasn't* here, we could?" A brief spark of heat passes between us with my question. A sharp breath hisses through her parted lips as her eyes flare wide.

I lean close, my lips inches from hers. "Could we?"

Ophie's exhale dances over my lips. "I mean"—she slips a hand along my side, her finger tugging the fabric of my shirt—"we *are* married."

She takes a step toward me, her body lining up with mine.

A loud clatter sounds from the other room, and we jump back as Sydney jerks awake. "I got it!"

There's another *thump* as she rolls off the chair to her hands and knees, grabbing for the wine glass on the ground. Ophie hurries over, bringing the towel she's been drying dishes with. Irritated at yet another interruption, I lean over the counter to see what's going on.

"Do you have soda water or carpet cleaner?" Sydney's words are fuzzy, but I can't tell if they're slurred or sleepy.

Ophie pulls her up off the floor. "Come on, Syd. Let's get you to bed. You can sleep here." She drapes Sydney's arm over her shoulder. "Philip? There's carpet cleaner under the sink. Can you...?"

Their voices carry as I spray and wipe the dribble of white wine before it soaks into the rug. After a few minutes, Ophie comes back out, looking over her shoulder as she joins me.

With a weary sigh, I stand up, crumpling the towel in my hand. "I guess I'm sleeping on the couch?"

"No, no. I'll sleep on the couch. I put her in my bed." She tries to take the bottle of cleaner from me, but I twist, keeping it out of her reach.

"You're not sleeping on the couch. I'll sleep out here."

"You don't fit on the couch."

"I fit just fine."

"No you don't, Philip. Don't be ridiculous."

"I'm not being ridiculous. You're being stubborn."

Again, she reaches out, and this time, she manages to snag the bottle out of my hand. Crowing in triumph, she scurries into the kitchen to put it away. I let her go, but as she rounds the counter toward me, I lean down and scoop her over my shoulder.

"Philip!"

"Shhhhh, you'll wake Sydney." I smack the back of her thighs but grab hold again when she starts sliding off. Between her squirming body and the loose sweatpants, we're both going to end up on the floor. "Stop it, or I'll drop you."

Ignoring my command, she keeps poking my back, her nails digging into my skin. "Philip, put me down. Put me down *now*."

I head toward my bedroom, swallowing my curse when my hip bashes into the back of the couch. "I'm not letting you take the couch. You should sleep in the bed, ninny."

"I'm not a ninny. You're a ninny. Besides, that's *your* bed." Her voice is muffled against my spine but still loud enough to hear.

"Didn't stop you from sleeping in it last night. Do you even know what a ninny is?" I push the door open and flick on the light, careful not to smack her head on the frame.

The bed is still half unmade, my side of the white duvet pushed aside from when I threw it back this morning. Ophie's side is perfectly neat, exactly how I found it this morning when I woke up and she was gone.

I turn to close the door behind me, not letting go of her thighs. "You sleep here. End of discussion."

"Only if you sleep here too." Being the stubborn woman she is, she wraps her arms around me in an upside-down koala hug. "I'm not letting go until you agree."

"You can't hang over my shoulder all night, Ophie."

"Watch me." She tightens her grip, her thighs tensing beneath my hands.

The challenge is too much to resist, so I lean forward, intending to toss her onto the bed. Instead of letting go and falling on her back like I expect, she keeps her death grip on me. As gravity takes over and she hits the bed at terminal velocity, she takes me with her.

I crash over her, my head and shoulder taking the brunt of my weight as they dig into her stomach. An unladylike noise trumpets from both her mouth and her ass as the rest of me rolls sideways off the edge of the bed. My butt catches on the corner, and the frame creaks ominously.

"Oh my god, oh my god." Ophie's horrified whispers meld with the noise of the bed frame cracking underneath us. With a final thud, my knees hit the ground as I roll off her. The silence that follows is deafening.

Ophie pushes up to her elbows. "Ahhh—"

"Did you—"

We both stop talking as the bed frame creaks again. Gingerly, I lift my elbows off the mattress. "Are you okay?" I try again after a moment of silence.

She doesn't answer, just stares at me, mouth open. It's dark, but I think her cheeks are turning red as I stare back.

"Ophie?"

She still doesn't respond, but her eyes are getting wider and wider. Just when I'm about to panic, she gasps and coughs, doubling over on the bed. Her sudden movement sets the bed groaning once more.

I push to my feet so I can check on her. As I get clear of the bed, it's obvious that the corner I hit is sitting lower than the rest of it.

"Did I knock the wind out of you?"

Ophie is still doubled over, gasping. I can't think of what else to do but rub circles on her back like a useless baboon. The creaking has stopped, so I keep rubbing her back as I lean down to inspect the damage.

The metal leg of the frame is bent at an angle, no longer supporting the weight of the bed. One good bounce on it would have the whole corner of the mattress sliding down like a waterfall.

"Fuck. I'm sorry, Ophie."

She finally catches her breath, curling up into a ball on her side, her one visible eye glaring at me. "We are never going to speak of this again."

"Speak of what?"

"Anything that happens in this room." Sucking a long breath in through her nose, she pushes up to her hands.

"You mean the sex? Or how you farted on my face?"

The second I say it, she bounces off the bed, but I catch her around the waist and pull her into me. The force of her back hitting my chest knocks me backward, the edge of the mattress catching the back of my knees and taking us down.

Again, we both fall onto the same corner as before. With a screech of metal, it collapses underneath us. Something under the bed breaks and splinters. We slide to the ground, the frame jabbing painfully into my spine, but I don't let go of my squirming wife.

"Philip, let me go." She pushes at me and kicks her legs, but I've got too good a grip.

"Only if you promise not to run away and wake up Sydney," I growl, desperate to let her go so I can relieve the pressure on my spine, but not wanting to let her escape and claim the couch.

No one is sleeping on the couch tonight if I have anything to say about it.

Ophie makes a few more attempts to escape before giving up. "Fine. But we're never going to mention it again." She collapses against me, and I let her slide off me. "Sorry."

"For farting on me? Or for being human?" I can't help it. I've only heard her fart once before, and I don't think she knows. Besides, reminding Ophie that she's a mere mortal is one of my favorite games.

"Ugh!" Red spreads across her cheeks before she covers her face with her hands, shaking her head. "Can you please let it go? It was not on purpose."

I want to let her squirm for another moment, but the curve of her neck is so tempting that it's only a few seconds before I break the silence. Leaning in close, I let my lips and nose trace the soft skin behind her ear and the back of her neck. "I barely even noticed."

She shivers as my lips pass over the bumps of her spine. "Philip..."

"Forget about it. I already have." I press my lips to her warm skin and watch the goose bumps rise in my wake. "I'll move out to Sunshine tomorrow. And it sounds like you're getting new roommates soon. I think we better make the most of our last night, don't you?"

She twists to look at me over her shoulder. "But...the bed? And Sydney's right there."

I press a kiss to her shoulder. "I can be quiet. Can you?"

Ophie

SOMEHOW, MAGGIE AND I managed to live together for years without me hearing her have sex in the other room. But she and Kel have been here less than two days, and I've already heard them three times.

Who knew being pregnant made you so horny? At least it's a great reminder for me not to test that theory for myself.

I roll over and grab my earbuds off the nightstand, stuffing them into my ears and flipping open Netflix on my phone to the first thing I see, hoping to stop the noise.

Thank god I had enough time to buy a new metal bed frame to replace the one Philip and I broke last week. And wash the sheets.

When sleep evades me, I pull out my laptop to see if any new magical job opportunities opened while I was sleeping. I scroll through half a dozen before one catches my eye. A start-up is looking for a shipping coordinator and project manager—it's an unusual combination and exactly what I'm looking for. A little internet sleuthing reveals they've just gotten venture capital funding, even more exciting. It's a marketplace for women-owned small businesses that helps them build their website storefronts and coordinates packaging and shipping for them. The more I read, the more excited I get about the opportunity. And it looks like the position would get to build the shipping and project management processes from scratch.

It's as if someone designed my dream job. Except for one thing—the position is in South Carolina. And there's no mention of it being remote.

I never considered leaving the West Coast. My family is here. Philip is here—for now. My life is here.

But the opportunity seems too good to pass up, even though I'm sure there are dozens of people more qualified than me applying. I take my time drafting a cover letter and fine-tuning my resume before submitting it, despite knowing it'll probably get fed to an algorithm and dropped to the bottom of a pile in thirty seconds.

I finally doze off again to the sounds of David Attenborough describing the cycle of life on prehistoric Earth, dreaming of the pastries I brought home with me after closing last night. The sun is blazing through my window when I open my eyes again, even though it's still early.

Thank god I have a couple hours before I need to get up and get ready for work.

Maggie is at her usual spot at the table, working on her laptop, when I emerge. Her keys click in a familiar cadence, one I've missed since she moved in with Kel.

"What's the story, Morning Glory?" A yawn interrupts my question as I pad across the floor to the kitchen.

"There's coffee in the pot. I think. And I hid your Danish in the microwave to keep it safe from Kel." She doesn't look up from her screen but points vaguely behind her.

"I appreciate your thoughtfulness."

"I'm the soul of consideration."

The coffee pot is still hot, so I pour myself a blessed mugful. "You weren't at three o'clock this morning." Leaning over, I pop open the microwave to check that the paper bag with my Danish is still there.

"I don't know what you're talking about." She grins at me over the edge of her mug, takes a sip, then grimaces and holds out her mug. "If there's any left, can you top me off?"

I grab the carafe and move to refill her mug. "Is this going to be a long-term solution to your commute? Should I invest in some sound-proofing?"

The microwave beeps before she answers, and I busy myself with getting my warm pastry on a plate, then join her at the table. "Seriously though, are you really going to keep living out at Sunshine? Aren't you both going to end up commuting into the city every day? That seems like a pain."

With a heavy sigh, she wraps her hands around her bright orange Tillamook mug. "Probably not. I actually think we're going to buy a place."

"Wow, that's a big step. I know I was a brat about you taking so damn long to finally get together, but shouldn't you maybe get married before you buy a house?"

My sister and Kel only started dating last fall, and it took forever for Kel to get his act together and ask Maggie out, but once they did, there was no looking back for either of them. I hate to admit that I'm maybe more than a little bit jealous of how smooth their relationship has been.

Not that I've put any effort into being in a relationship myself—I have Philip, after all. What else do I need?

Maggie is the only person who knows the full story behind my vow not to date in grad school. She'd been the one to pick me up from my narcissistic college boyfriend's house in the middle of the night after I found out he'd given me and half of Gamma Gamma Delta chlamydia. She'd held my hand at the pharmacy while I'd waited for my antibiotics and Plan B prescriptions, and been the one to keep me company as I frantically studied to make up my grades when I'd been too scared to go to class after his threatening texts.

I don't have the excuse of being in school anymore when my family gets on my case about being single. If only I could find something as easy and straightforward as she has.

She lets me get a couple of bites in while she types on her laptop before she answers. "Eh. I think we might wait until I'm less pregnant and more excited at the prospect."

Furrowing my brow, I twist my head to stare at my sister. "But you love weddings. How are you not excited to plan your own?"

I've watched Maggie plan her own wedding a million times since we were little. "Is it because of Frank?" Her ex-fiancé was a douche, but it wasn't like he left her at the altar.

"No. But Nate and Sydney still refuse to be in the same room as each other. I'm exhausted. Jackie and Greg are gone for a few more months, and by the time they get back, I'm going to be feeling more bridge troll than bridal."

She leans back in her chair, circling her wrists and tipping her head from side to side, stretching out her neck. "Honestly? Philip taking over the tasting room will be a huge help. Kel still feels responsible for Sunshine, and having Nate's grumpy ass chasing away customers while Jackie is gone has him eating antacids like candy."

"But can I help *you* somehow? I thought pregnancy was supposed to make you all glowy and shit, but your black circles have black circles."

A dash of hope flickers across her face as she flips her laptop toward me. There's a spreadsheet open with rows and rows of vendors, addresses, dates, and times. None of it lines up or makes sense. It's as if she's scribbled in a notebook in the spreadsheet.

"I don't suppose you can make heads or tails of this?"

"Gimme, gimme!" I reach my grabby hands out to start cleaning up her spreadsheet. But horror dawns as I scan the page. "Jesus, Maggie, what is this even tracking?"

It's okay. I can fix this.

We spend the morning walking through her mess and transferring it into a series of organized sheets. I even have the joy of creating a few pivot tables for her.

"You're a lifesaver, Ophie. I wish I could afford to hire you to keep me organized." She sighs as she leans back in her chair.

I push back from the table, my stomach growling from three hours of spreadsheet fun. "I'll keep you organized for free, Mags. But first, lunch."

Pushing to her feet, she joins me in the kitchen. She shoves me away from the fridge and pulls out a box of leftover Chinese food. "Have you considered seeing if there's a position at Mailbox? Or if Sutton could put in a good word for you somewhere?"

"Maggie, I am not going to ask Theodore Sutton to 'put in a good word for me.' I barely know him. Besides, Mailbox is a strictly digital product. My degree is in global shipping and trade—it's not the same thing."

Shaking her ass in a little dance, my sister dumps the contents of the cardboard box onto a plate, a combination of chow mein, fried rice, and cashew chicken, then pops it into the microwave before turning to give me a look. "Yeah, but you told me that your degree is basically a really advanced project management certification? Surely, he knows someone who could use that kind of skill."

I roll my eyes. I swear, she's never met a stranger. I don't know how she can walk up to people and just...yap at them until they give her what she wants.

"I still barely know the man, and he definitely would never remember me. There is no way on earth he's going to just give me a job." I pause. "Philip probably has more of the kind of skills Sutton needs. He complained all the time, but I know for a fact he had a 4.0 GPA in all his finance classes."

The beeping microwave interrupts her before she can argue. I stall further argument by plating my food and taking it out on the patio to eat. I can hear her talking to herself as she does the same, but she falls quiet as she sits down in the chair beside me.

The porch is just big enough for the pair of Adirondack chairs Maggie rescued from a garage sale the summer after we moved in. We had plants out here at one point, but we had a huge ice storm this winter and Maggie had been stuck out at Sunshine with Kel for a week. I'd holed up inside with the heat, taking my classes over Zoom, and by the time I'd thought about the plants, they had been beyond saving.

"I assumed Philip was heading back to South Africa after graduation." Maggie slides back into her chair with a grunt.

I shove some rice into my mouth before I answer, the hot and salty food exactly what I needed after staring at her laptop screen all morning. "There's nothing for him to go back to. His brother and parents are in Australia now. And I quote, 'The only thing left for me in Cape Town is a stage-five clinger of an ex-girlfriend and an economy that will never catch up to the rest of the world.'"

She laughs, a piece of rice shooting across the porch to land in front of the hopeful robin that'd been watching us from a nearby bush. It makes her snort even harder, and soon, we're both laughing ourselves silly over our lunch. "Oh my god, do you remember that time Daisy shot milk out of her nose? I've never seen her turn so red." Maggie is still giggling.

"I think it's still the only time I've ever seen her be anything but perfect." My own giggles interrupt my words, but she nods in understanding.

"God, she really is annoyingly perfect, isn't she?"

"I don't know if I'd call it annoying. More like intimidating."

When she gives me a funny look, I shove more food into my mouth so I don't have to elaborate on how I've always been a little afraid of our oldest sister.

"Did I ever tell you about the time she accidentally dyed her hair purple?"

"What? No. How did I not know this?"

"She was trying to brighten her blond and used too much purple shampoo." Maggie lets out one of her belly laughs at the memory. I've always envied her ability to laugh like that—like she doesn't give a fuck who hears her.

"How come I don't remember this?"

"It was one of the summers we went to nationals for dance—you were probably home with Dad doing summer school."

"Hmph." I lean back in my seat, remembering all the summers my older sisters would go away for dance stuff. If it wasn't nationals, it was a camp. Or a convention. One year, Maggie was gone for four weeks at a ballet intensive. Even though I knew at the age of seven that it was not for me, I was always so jealous of the time the two of them got to spend with Mom doing dance stuff. Dad and I would hang out doing crossword puzzles or watching movies when I was younger. By the time I was in high school and spending my summers practicing for academic decathlon, I'd talked myself into believing that all the time they spent dancing was a waste.

Now I'm not so sure. It seems like they had a lot more fun together growing up than I did.

"Did she get in trouble?"

Maggie laughs. "Of course not. She showered, like, ten times before our dance teacher saw her. All the gel and hairspray makes your hair look dark anyway, so Miss Tanya didn't notice until we were on stage for awards."

We fall into silence as we finish eating. Birds chirp at us from the greenbelt behind the condo, fighting to be heard over the cars and trucks passing by on the main road.

With a sigh, Maggie sets down her empty plate. "You know, there are times I really miss the sound of civilization." A fire engine goes by, sirens blaring. "And other times I don't. You wouldn't believe how quiet it is out at Sunshine when the tasting room is closed and the sun goes down."

"Can't say I've ever experienced it."

"You should go and stay with Philip one night while he's out there and see for yourself. It's wild." She pauses, then casually changes the subject so fast I nearly choke. "He's such a good guy, Ophie. If he's not going back to South Africa, I don't understand why you two aren't together."

Anger flares in my chest so fast that I snap at my sister without thinking. "I'm so tired of people asking me that. He's my best friend. We aren't dating. Leave it alone."

Pushing to my feet, I swipe our plates and stalk into the kitchen. I love my sister, I do. But if one more person insists on telling me what I should do with my love life, I'm going to scream.

Why can't anyone else see that *of course* I'm head over fucking heels for the man, but he's leaving me one way or another—either to go to

Australia or somewhere else in the country that offers him a job. He hates the Pacific Northwest.

Philip is sunshine and citrus, yoga at the beach, and flip-flops—or thongs, as he calls them—year-round.

I'm sweaters and hot cocoa, hikes in the rain, and forgetting to shave my legs for a month because I live in sweatpants.

His happily ever after doesn't include me, and I refuse to hurt him by making him break my heart.

Philip

I haven't seen Ophie for over a week and it's slowly driving me insane. Working at Sunshine has been a great distraction, but I keep comparing every woman who comes in to Ophie. Not even spending hours every morning submitting job applications to every place I can find has been enough to stop me from wondering what she's doing all day.

And missing our usual constant texting. My phone has been suspiciously silent for the last few days, and I suspect it has to do with her having second thoughts about our marital relations the other night. And the night after.

The couple I've been pouring for decides on a bottle and takes it outside on the patio to drink as the sun dips toward golden hour. I have to admit that I'm having fun working here. Pouring wine for people looking to relax and enjoy their afternoon is the opposite of high stress. And the view doesn't suck either.

Nate slips in the back door with a case balanced on his shoulder and a scowl on his face. "I saw we were running low on the Estate Pinot. You doing okay with the POS?"

I take the case from him and set it on the floor so we can both reach inside. Pulling out two bottles, I slide them into the rack beside Nate's two. "Yeah, man, the till is good. Thanks for bringing those in. The Amelia has also been popular today, so we'll probably need to bring up some more tonight."

"I heard you telling people it was named after my grandmother. You know it was named after a cat, right?" Nate grumbles the words before giving me a testy look.

"You guys had a cat?" I raise my eyebrow and grab another pair of bottles. "I've heard of winery dogs, but not cats."

A soft smile I've never seen before graces his face. "It was Kel and Sydney's cat. Sydney's, really, but since her mom is allergic, it lived here." His smile drops as soon as he notices me watching. "It would cuddle with just about anyone. And it was good at killing snakes."

From the way he doesn't make any more conversation or eye contact, I get the feeling there's more to this story than he's letting on. But anytime I even open my mouth about anything other than the fucking POS system, he clams up.

"If it doesn't bother you, I think I'll stick to my story about your grandmother. It's a little more poetic than a snake-killing cat." I pause, then give Nate a grin. "Okay, well, I'll save the killer-cat stories for the people who look like they might enjoy it."

Shaking his head, he stacks the empty box with the rest of the ones we keep on hand for customers. "You do you. Just sell the wine."

He turns to leave but stops in the empty doorway. "Hey, you're going to help us with the winery tour event next week, right?"

I lean back against the bar, arms crossed, and one foot kicked over the other. "Yup."

"I'll give you a tour tomorrow morning so you only have to bullshit your way through half of it. Meet me outside at seven."

He's gone before I have a chance to negotiate for a later start time, disappearing out the door with a wave of heat. A second wave drifts in from the opposite side as a group of women and a pair of dogs enter the tasting room.

They span a motley of ages, the youngest looking about twenty and the oldest in the "I don't dare ask, but I'll card her to make her smile" range. The pair of corgis with them have their noses stuck in the air to sniff. I swear one of them is already eyeing the salami hidden in the fridge.

"Ladies, welcome. And who are these adorable pups with you?"

I'm busy with customers until well after we're supposed to close—the group of women lingering by the bar as I close out. There's a scuffle between two of the ones who have been fairly quiet—a curvier woman with long brown hair and a shorter, slender woman with red hair who pushes her toward the bar.

When she doesn't do anything except smile at me, the slender one makes an exasperated noise and joins her. "We've been debating where your accent is from all afternoon. My friend thinks it's Cape Town, but I think it's Durban. Care to help us settle a bet?"

I grin, setting down the glass in my hand. "It's not often people even get the country right without asking me. How come you're both so well-versed in the colonial English accent? And what's the prize for the winner?"

The women look at each other, the shorter one grinning when the other one's eyes go wide and panicked. Then, her grin turning flirtatious, she turns to me, setting her elbows on the counter and pressing her boobs together.

Now I understand the game they're playing.

"Winner gets to give you her number." She winks, keeping that smile aimed at me.

A vision of Ophie flirting with me like that flashes across my mind, sending a wave of warmth through my belly and softening my shoulders. The short one mistakes the change in my posture for reciprocal flirting and starts to twirl a piece of hair around her finger.

"So? Is either of us right?" Again, she shifts her shoulders, but I keep my eyes away from her cleavage.

I lean forward, then shift to my left so I'm facing her friend. "Cape Town, born and raised." Her bright blue eyes flare impossibly wider, but before she can say anything, I keep talking. "And while I appreciate your appreciation, I'm a married man and thus, must politely decline your kind offer."

I finish with a little flourish and a bow, sliding their empty glasses off the counter as I straighten, then turning to put them in the collection bin. When I turn back, the shy friend is smiling and looking relieved, while the spicy one has her hands on her hips, glaring at me.

"You don't have a wedding ring on," Spicy Spice points out, lips pursed.

I hold up my left hand. "Doesn't make me any less married."

She humphs and flounces away to the other women, throwing me one last annoyed look over her shoulder as she goes. I chuckle to myself as she walks away, dimly aware of the click of the back door closing.

"Your wife's a lucky girl." The shy one finally speaks. "And don't mind my friend, she flirts for sport."

I pause in my tidying to chat. "I would say that I'm the lucky one. She deserves the world and somehow ended up with me."

"How did you guys meet?" She taps her fingers on the bar as she speaks—maybe it's a nervous tic, maybe just a habit. Either way, it reminds me of Ophie and her pens. "Seriously, because you seem like a genuinely good guy, and they seem to be impossible to find these days. I'm pretty sure between us"—she points at Spicy—"we've swiped through every available man in a fifty-mile radius on every dating app."

"We met on the first day of grad school, and she's been my best friend ever since. We only got married a couple months ago, right before graduation."

I'm startled by the tinkling of glasses toppling. With a jerk, I turn around, expecting to find a disaster, maybe a wild corgi behind the bar, but it's just Nate. He hoists the bin of dirty glasses to his shoulder and walks away without a word.

I turn back to my conversation companion, who's watching Nate leave, her eyes glued to his ass, her bottom lip caught between her teeth.

I chuckle. "Don't even think about it. He makes a piranha look friendly."

She doesn't take her eyes off him until he disappears into the tiny kitchen area. "But I like them tall, dark, and broody. Unfortunately," she adds with a shake of her head.

"He's not broody, he's just mean," I counter. "But I shouldn't say that since, technically, he's my boss."

"Your wife is a lucky woman." Her friends call from the doorway, and she steps away from the bar to join them, waving goodbye as she leaves.

I follow behind to lock the door and finish cleaning up. As nice as they were, talking about Ophie with those women made the niggle in my chest that misses her worse.

I'm still thinking about her when I finish up and walk down to the cabin I'm staying in. Greg and Jackie's little one-bedroom place is cozy and overrun with chickens. Not real chickens, but rooster statues. There's rooster dinner wear, roosters on the throw pillows, and even roosters on the very nineties-looking border wallpaper. I was stunned when Nate said the three cabins down here had only been built six years ago. I thought they had just renovated a much older place.

When I step inside, I know I must really be losing it because I swear I can smell my wife's shampoo.

"Kel came home with a giant tub of whipped cream and a look in his eye that said I wasn't going to get any sleep tonight, so I hope you don't mind that I'm here," the source of the scent calls from the rooster-covered kitchen. "And just in case you are annoyed about it...I already started cooking dinner, so you can't kick me out."

I clear the entryway and spy Ophie in the kitchen, stirring something in a pot. "If that's tomato soup I smell, then you can stay as long as there are grilled cheese sandwiches to go with it. And please don't put Kel and whipped cream together in a sentence ever again."

"Trust me," Ophie says, looking back over her shoulder, "they are not words I wanted to put together in my mind either."

Her tone is teasing, but her shoulders are stiff, and she keeps dropping her eyes to the floor. A strange tension hangs in the air between us, the echo of a conversation we never had after the other night.

I wrap one hand around her waist to hug her from the side. She keeps stirring, attention glued to the soup. "I didn't think you liked grilled cheese and tomato soup, but either way, I can't make it with you holding me." She drawls out "to-*mah*-to" with a terrible impression of my accent, making me grin despite the awkwardness.

"Hi to you too. It's one of the weird American combinations that you've tricked me into appreciating. I still stand firm that peanut butter and chocolate is an atrocity against food." I dodge the elbow she jabs at me, still holding on. "My day was fine, by the way. Flirted with a few women, met a couple of corgis. Got some juicy gossip on Nate and Sydney. How was yours?"

Ophie twists until she's facing me, the tomato soup-covered wooden spoon in her hand dangerously close to smacking me in the face. "Carb, tomato, and cheese. It's a classic combination that is *always* good, so don't make it into some weird American thing." She starts counting off on her fingers. "Pizza, lasagna, enchiladas—should I go on?"

I laugh and let go so I can take the spoon from her. "Okay, okay. I concede the point. Go make me a sammich, Mrs. van der Merwe."

"Ahem."

My heart picks up speed when Ophie doesn't react to the name like she usually does.

"Please?" I add when she doesn't move.

She waves her hand away. "You said you had gossip. I want to know."

She's not even going to acknowledge that I called her Mrs.? Have I entered the Twilight Zone? My heart and stomach are flipping between racing and dropping at her non-reaction.

I grab the wooden spoon and stir the soup, needing something to do with my hands while she pulls cheese out of the fridge and starts assembling sandwiches.

"Um, yeah." I have to tear my eyes away from the long line of her neck as she bends over her task. She's wearing a yellow sundress that hits her mid-thighs, with short sleeves that flutter around her arms as she spreads butter on the bread.

She bought it last summer for Cassie's birthday party. I remember because I went shopping with her to pick it out. At the time, I'd thought it looked amazing on her but hadn't really noticed just how low the front dipped between her breasts because I'd been too busy lusting over a leather jacket for myself that I could never afford.

Now, the dress is screaming at me to see how easily I can get my hands beneath it.

Clearing my throat, I refocus on stirring the bubbling red liquid in the pot. "So, you know the Amelia? The riesling?"

"Oh, I like that one. What does that have to do with Nate and Sydney and their weird tension?"

I reach into the cupboard beside me and set a pan on the burner next to mine, turning it on to heat for the sandwiches. "He overheard me telling some guests that it was named after his grandmother and corrected me that it was actually named after Sydney's cat."

"He named a wine after her cat?"

"That's what he said. And he almost smiled."

Ophie turns to face me, the assembled sandwiches forgotten on the counter behind her. "He *smiled*?"

"Well, it was more like he ceased scowling for a moment. Which, for Nate, is a downright cheerful expression."

Laughing at my joke, she brings the sandwiches over and sets them in the sizzling pan. Any lingering awkwardness fades with the sound. Even though all I want to do is get my hands under that dress, the annoying pinch in my chest from missing her all week eases. And the tension in my spine fades away at the sound of my best friend's laugh.

Ophie's shoulders are relaxed as she moves to stand beside me. Her hip bumps mine and our elbows clash. Dropping my spoon into the pot, I step back to make more space for her, unable to resist gripping her hips as I do.

But right then, she leans forward, her ass grazing my crotch, and I suck in a breath at the contact, tightening my hold on her hips. The fabric of her dress bunches under my fingers as I pull myself together. A different kind of tension rockets through my body, and now I'm afraid to breathe wrong in case it breaks something precious.

Instead of straightening her ramrod spine like I expect, her body goes soft. "I don't want to burn dinner," she murmurs while leaning back, her weight settling against me with a sigh. My brain short-circuits, any conversation I thought we needed cut off at the knees by her body language.

Slowly, I gather more of the fabric in my fingers, pulling the dress higher and higher on her thighs. I dip my head down to speak low in her ear. "Who said anything about burning dinner?"

My lips are so close, I can't tell if the taste of her in my mouth is real or from my memories of the other night. The warmth of her skin tickles my lips at her neck and my fingertips on her thighs. My thumbs brush the edge of her panties, and I hesitate to go further.

We stay like that—my mouth millimeters from her skin, my fingers brushing the crease of her hip, the only sounds her hitched breathing—for an agonizing collection of heartbeats.

I want more than anything to hook my fingers in her underwear and pull them down to her knees, but I have no idea if that's what she wants. Her body is telling me yes, but just because she was okay with this while we were living together doesn't mean she's okay with it now.

I would be lying to myself if I didn't want some reassurance that she missed me as much as I missed her. That I'm not the only one overwhelmed by the idea of an us that means more than just a platonic partnership.

"I can hear you thinking from here," Ophie huffs.

"I—"

"How am I the one who's not overthinking this? Overthinking is *my* specialty, not yours." She bends her head to the side, giving me more access to her neck and shoulder. Slowly, not breaking the contact between us, she reaches out and turns off the burners on the stove. Her hands drift back and settle on top of mine, pressing my fingertips deeper into her skin.

I want to melt from her warmth, sink to my knees and taste her, but the smooth expanse of her shoulder calls to me just as loudly. Leaning down, I drag my lips across the shell of her ear, into the space behind it, then along her neck to bite down on the tendon where her shoulder joins.

Ophie moans as I press my teeth into her skin, the sound bypassing the rational part of my brain and arrowing straight to the animal bit that's been chanting "mine, mine, mine" since the day we met.

"Fuck, Ophie. Are you—"

Flipping around, she slaps a hand across my mouth. "Don't."

Our bodies are pressed together, her breasts crushed against my chest, her hips lined up against mine, the sundress caught between us. Without breaking eye contact, I wrap my fingers around her wrist and pull her hand away from my mouth. Twisting her arm behind her back, I pin it there with my hand. The motion pulls at the soft fabric of her dress, the deep V in front exposing half of her breast.

"For the last time, Philip. We're both adults. I already told you I wanted this. What else is there to discuss?"

There is so much more to discuss. Is this just casual to her? Or does it mean more? As close as we've been for the last two years, the one topic we never discussed was how we feel about sex. Maybe because it would have meant admitting we were ignoring something vital between us in the name of safety.

But right now, my beautiful best friend is staring up at me, her eyes dilated with lust, her lips parted and begging for me to nibble on them. Any remnants of self-control I've been holding on to snap. I push all my overthinking aside and scoop her up, wrapping her legs around my hips.

"Couch or bedroom?" I slide my hands beneath her ass, backing us out of the kitchen and away from the heat still coming off the range.

"Couch is closer." Ophie points behind me before diving in and capturing my lips with hers.

"God, I missed your mouth." I walk us to the couch, a giant L-shaped thing that's too big for this place but obviously well-loved. She doesn't stop kissing me as I release her legs and ease us down into the corner. Instead, her tongue invades my mouth and her hands attack my shirt.

Pulling it over my head breaks our frantic kiss. Immediately, Ophie's hands roam over my chest as I toss it to the side. "How are you so tan?" Her question ends in a squeak as I pull her hips toward me. Her feet are planted on the floor, her knees draped over my shoulders, that dress just barely covering her sweet pussy.

"It's summer." I shrug, then hook my fingers in the edge of her panties and pull. I take a moment to admire the smooth skin of her inner thighs, the pink lips of her core peeking out. "Mmm, I've been missing this tasty treat."

Ophie lies back with a little laugh. "It's so hard to take you seriously when you dirty talk..."

I ignore her and dive in, running the tip of my nose between her folds. "You were saying?" I follow with my tongue, laying the flat of it against her pussy and licking up her length, slow and firm.

"I'm going to be quiet now," she whispers to the ceiling. "Just don't stop doing that."

"But I like it when you talk." I squeeze her thighs as I repeat the action, slowing down when her legs finally relax. "And don't worry, I remember all the spots that made you scream last time."

"You're like an elephant." Ophie giggles as she settles into the couch, talking to the ceiling as I go to work, licking and sucking, listening for the same sounds she made before. "And I didn't scream last time. I was being quiet so we didn't wake up Sydney."

I don't answer, too busy using my teeth to nibble along the inside of her thigh while my finger takes the place of my tongue.

Ophie keeps up a litany of nonsense as I work her body. "I can't believe we broke the bed. Although, I suppose the frame was pretty old. It was Daisy's from our parents' house. Maggie took it when she moved in with me after Frank broke off their—"

"Liefling?" I finally pull myself away from her hot center. "If you're still talking about your sister's bed frame, I am obviously not doing this right."

Lifting her head, she gives me a guilty smile. "Sorry. You are definitely doing it right. I got..."

"Nervous?"

"Not exactly. It's just easier not to think about the fact that you're...you."

I sit back on my heels. "Ophie, we don't have to do this."

My cock will never forgive me for saying that.

"That's kind of what I came over for, though. I don't know, Philip. I don't know what's wrong with me." She tucks her feet under her and sits up. "When you're not with me, all I can think about is how great the sex was and how much I want to do it again. But when you're actually here and, well, doing it, I get all up in my head about if this is a good idea or not."

She crisscrosses her legs on the couch, which is painfully tempting, but I force my eyes to stay locked on her face. "I don't want to just fuck," she adds in a voice so quiet it's only audible because there is zero ambient noise out here.

I pinch her chin and pull her head down so I can press a kiss to her forehead. "I don't really know what we're doing, but I know it's not just fucking."

Ophie looks up at me as I pull back, a calculating look in her eye. "What happens at Sunshine stays at Sunshine?"

I tip my head to the side. "What does that mean?"

"This doesn't change the fact that we have no idea where we're going to end up in a few months—you might get a job anywhere. But for now, anything that we do here, well...it just means that we're both here and it feels good, and there's nothing long-term to it."

"Just marriage."

Ophie shakes her head. "That's insurance." She waves a hand, but I catch her wrist.

"No fucking anyone else, though."

Her tinkling laugh fills the room as she takes an exaggerated look around the cabin. "Who else is there? Nate?" She makes a face. "No fucking anyone else."

It's not the conversation I really wanted, but it will do for now. Enough to stop me from second-guessing if she wants this or not. My dick goes hard at the idea of finally getting to claim Ophie without constantly worrying about the consequences.

Instead of letting my brain take over again, I scoop her up and carry her to the bedroom, our lips tangled and her legs wrapped tight around my hips. Her dress and my clothes are on the floor moments later. It takes only seconds for me to grab a condom from the pack in my bag, sheath myself, and climb over her.

Ophie blinks up at me, her eyes soft, her body stretched out beneath me. "Come here."

She reaches up and pulls me into a kiss. Her hands slide into my hair, holding me in place as her hips rock against mine. Matching her rhythm, I nestle my dick between her thighs and deepen the kiss, pulling on her bottom lip with my teeth.

I release her lip before pressing kisses across her cheek to her jaw. Holding myself up on one elbow, I guide myself to her entrance and push in, groaning as her warmth envelops me.

"That feels so good," Ophie says to the ceiling while I continue exploring her neck and chest with my mouth.

Running my hand along the side of her body, I marvel at the softness of my best friend. She presents herself as so put together, as someone who always knows what they're doing and how. It's not surprising I've felt a need to make her a little messy since the day we met. But now, I don't just want to see her a little frazzled. Now, I have a burning need to watch her unravel beneath me. To make her feel so good, she couldn't hold on to her self-control no matter how much she wanted to.

If her stream of consciousness as I massage her breast and drag myself in and out of her is anything to go by, I think I might be pretty close to making her lose control. "God, I love how vocal you are," I murmur into her ear, taking her earlobe between my teeth.

Her only response is a gasp as I piston my hips a little faster, letting the friction between us build, and the tingle of an orgasm travels up from my toes.

"Is that good? Do I feel as good for you as you feel for me?" I ask more questions, urging her to keep talking. For once, her words tumble free without being checked by her filter or needing to say the right thing. I set a steady pace, digging my pelvis down into her clit at the bottom of each thrust.

"Do that again," she moans when I pinch her nipple. "Please, Philip."

Hearing her say my name is the reassurance my soul needed—knowing that she was here by choice, on purpose—and my body takes over. I throw one of her legs over my shoulder, using my knees and the new angle to slide deeper and deeper inside her. Branding her from the inside, and knowing I've loved her since the day I met her, even if I didn't realize it.

My pending explosion gathers in my spine, all the muscles in my back screaming that we're close, so close. I'm holding off my orgasm by a thread, needing her to fall over the edge with me as I keep the pace.

"Come on, baby. Come for me." I need her to fall apart soon, or else I'm going to have to go back to tasting her sweet pussy so I don't disgrace myself.

Ophie tightens around me, her nails clawing at my back and arms as she arches against me, her head thrown back while she cries out. I keep going, not slowing down as she rides out her orgasm. With a groan, I bite down on the muscle between her neck and shoulder. My vision goes black for a second, the unstoppable wave of my release hitting me.

Both of us gasping for breath, I roll off and flop beside her so I can remove the condom and tie it off, dropping it into the small trash can beside the bed. She reaches up to stroke my cheek with the tips of her fingers. "That was..." She pauses and takes two deep breaths. "Good. So good."

She's grinning, so I'm pretty sure that *good* really means great, but I scrunch my face anyway, feigning hurt. "Just good? Pretty sure Nate heard you all the way in his cabin."

Ophie laughs and smacks my chest. "Talking about Nate, or anyone else, within ninety seconds of orgasm is against the rules. Now you've ruined my high."

I laugh, pulling her against my chest. My stomach rumbles, but I ignore it so I can enjoy the sensation of holding my Ophie without worrying about where my hands are. "I won't do it again, I promise, my liefling."

"I've always wondered what that means." As she wiggles, her asspresses against me.

"It means something nice." I dodge giving her a straight answer by kissing the back of her neck and running my fingers down the outside of her thigh. She's going to jerk away in a second when I hit her ticklish spot.

Right on cue, Ophie shrieks and flails, and I roll off the bed behind her and dart away before she can retaliate. "Where's the dinner I was promised? You taste delicious, but I'm still hungry."

Ophie

Maggie was right. It's so quiet out here, my thoughts are echoing around my brain with nothing to drown them out.

I squeeze the mug in my hands as I stare out over the mist-covered vines, my warm coffee chasing off the slight early morning chill. It's August, and even though it's supposed to be in the nineties today, it won't get hot until much later. Right now, the wooden porch is cold under my bare feet, and my exposed arms are covered in goose bumps.

Jackie and Greg's cabin, the one Philip and I are staying in, is closest to the tasting room—Nate's, then Maggie and Kel's sitting downhill from us. Kel's cabin is dark and silent, but a square patch of light shines on the ground from one of Nate's windows.

I let the quiet wash over me, broken only by the sound of Philip getting ready to meet Nate for his seven a.m. tour. The eerie view and sounds of nature are a balm to my bruised feelings. Our clandestine rendezvous have been simultaneously hot as fuck and sweet as sugar, but they always leave me feeling a little more broken inside. That's why I had to take a break from him last week—I needed a moment to nurse my breaking heart. How will I bear it when he inevitably leaves me?

Or I leave him.

I had every intention of pulling out my laptop to reread the email from Penny Zimmerman to interview for the position at her start-up in South Carolina, but I can't risk Philip seeing it. I haven't brought myself to say anything about it to him yet. We changed the rules of our friendship knowing there was a good chance of this happening, but now that the reality of it is here, I would do anything to put off seeing his face at the news.

I'd much rather pretend that we can live in this bubble forever.

Instead of reading the email for the hundredth time, I let the misty morning and bird calls draw me outside. I can see why Maggie likes it out here, although I imagine between her and Olive, the quiet isn't as oppressive, broken by their constant chatter. No wonder Kel loves having her there.

Some kind of large bird calls out in the distance. When no animal calls back, it repeats a few times. It's a lonely sound—kind of how I felt before Philip. He had no idea how anxious and alone I felt that first day of classes, before he sat beside me and immediately started teasing me.

The way I felt growing up, watching my older sisters share a bond that excluded me, is completely foreign to him. Even though it was my choice not to share in it, watching the two of them head off to dance every afternoon while I stayed home, or sat in the car doing homework while they were inside, built an invisible wall between us. A wall that only started to come down when Daisy went to college, and by then, it was hard to break the habit of loneliness.

I was so used to being alone that having other people in my life felt oppressive, even as I craved it.

I turn at the sound of the front door opening.

"Your phone is ringing." Philip crosses the porch, stealing my mug from me. "Oh bless, that's good."

"There's a whole pot inside—you could have your own mugful." I make a face at him.

"But I like the way you make it better." He punctuates his statement by slurping down a mouthful, dancing in place as his eyes water.

"Too hot?" I laugh as he struggles to swallow, his eyes bulging.

"Just a smidge. Here." He pushes the mug back into my hands, then starts to walk away. "Wish me luck with old When-we."

"When-we?"

Philip laughs, tucking his hands into his pockets before he strolls toward Nate's cabin. "'When we did it in France...,' 'when we were in charge...,' 'when my dad...'" He shakes his head. "It's what we call the old Rhodies and Afrikaners. The ones who can't let go of when they were in charge."

"That's actually perfect." I shake my head. "Good luck with old When-we," I call out as Philip trots away laughing.

I can't see him anymore, but his voice drifts back, calling out a greeting to Nate. The sound of their conversation fades as I stand there, sipping the hot drink. I snort. "When-we. More like When-Sydney-finally-tells-me-what-the-hell-the-story-is."

I make my way inside, ready to pull out my laptop and write another mind-numbing cover letter. At least I don't have to work at the coffee shop today. Picking up my phone, I flinch at the dozen notifications from various job-hunting sites that flash at me from the screen. I spend the morning working through them one at a time, hesitating every time the location is outside of the Pacific Northwest, but also determined not to change my life plans just because I have *feelings*.

My stomach is rumbling as I go back to Penny's email one last time.

Dear Ophelia, First of all, let me apologize for originally scheduling your interview at six in the morning. I'm on the East Coast and forgot about the time difference! Thank you for being gracious about my blunder. I am very excited to sit down and chat with you next week. In order to prepare for your interview, it would be helpful if you could complete the following questionnaire...

I'm still mulling the questionnaire over when my phone rings. Cassie's voice greets me as I hit the button. "Hey, hermit, what are you doing?"

"Hello to you too." I laugh, sitting back on the couch and closing my laptop.

"Pfft. I haven't seen you in weeks."

"You were on your honeymoon, remember?"

"We got back three days ago."

"Wow, three whole days back and you're already sick of TJ? That doesn't bode well for your marriage," I tease, tucking my feet underneath the blanket on the end of the couch.

Cassie laughs. "Hardly. But I miss my friend, too."

I smile at that. Cassie has always been a good friend to me, putting up with my hermit ways and only complaining occasionally when I invite Philip to everything. "I missed you too. How was Mexico?"

"I'll tell you about it over drinks. You want to meet me at the waterfront?"

I look around the cabin, not loving the idea of driving across the river to Vancouver and back. "I'm actually staying out at Sunshine Cellars. Do you want to come down here? The tasting room opens in an hour."

"Why are you there?"

"Long story short, Maggie and Kel kind of moved back into my place, and I couldn't take the sound of them having sex another night."

Cassie laughs so loud I have to hold the phone away from my ear. "Okay, I for sure don't ever want to think about your sister having sex again, but that is hilarious. I'll be there at noon, and I want to know everything."

As soon as I hang up the call, I head to the bathroom to take a shower. The hot water running down my back reminds me of the way Philip had run his fingers down my spine as we were falling asleep last night, my head pillowed on his chest.

"Hulloo," Philip calls out as I step out of the shower. "Ophie?"

"In the bedroom," I call back, wrapping a towel around my body and tucking it in. I grab another one and flip my head over, twisting it around my wet hair.

He bounds into the room as I straighten, a grin on his face. A grin that turns a little predatory when he sees me. "Hello, hello. Is it lunchtime already?"

"Are you hungry? I can make sandwiches if you give me a minute."

Philip just grins even wider and takes my hand, pulling me over to the bed. "That's not what I'm hungry for."

With that, he pushes me back, the edge of the bed catching my knees and forcing me to sit. In an instant, he's kneeling between my thighs, his hands guiding them apart.

Fifteen minutes later, we're both flushed and damp. My pussy has been thoroughly devoured, and the salty taste of Philip's cum still coats my mouth. "You better hurry and get dressed." I push his shoulder as he lies beside me on the bed.

"In a mo. Need to check my limbs are all still attached first." He turns his head to the side and smiles. "Ophie—"

I pop off the bed before he can say anything else. If he's going to say sweet things, I'll never be able to let him go once his visa is safe. Better to keep things light. "Cassie is on her way. She's meeting me at the tasting room for a drink."

"Is TJ coming too?" He takes the hint and rolls off the bed, picking his discarded pants up from the floor and shaking the legs right side out.

I rummage through my overnight bag, looking for underwear and a bra. "Nope. Just a girls' gossip session, as far as I know."

"I'll be on the lookout for trouble from you two." He pulls a clean shirt out of his suitcase. "Are you going to tell her about us?"

I freeze, my bra still backward on my chest. "No? I thought we were keeping this quiet. That's still the plan, right?" I twist my bra around so I can finish putting it on, waiting for Philip to say something. He still hasn't responded by the time I get it straight, the straps untwisted and my boobs sitting in the cups correctly. "Philip?"

His eyes are glued to my body. "Do you always put your bra on like that? It's like scooping ice cream."

"You didn't answer my question," I point out, pulling a jersey dress out of my bag. I love sundresses; they make getting dressed so easy.

Philip groans. "Are you really going to wear that?"

I smooth the orange fabric down over my hips, twisting from side to side so it flares out. "Why? What's wrong with it?"

"I'm going to be imagining what's underneath it all afternoon."

I roll my eyes and take my bag of toiletries to the bathroom to finish getting ready. "You still didn't answer my question."

He sneaks in behind me and turns on the shower. "I was not planning to say anything to Cassie. Or TJ. Or our families." He sticks his hand under the water to test the temperature, then steps in, his backside disappearing under the steam before I can reach back to squeeze it. "Nate, uh, may suspect, though."

I squeeze a bit of sunscreen on my fingers, rubbing it into my skin as I speak. "Do we care what Nate thinks? And would he tell anyone?"

His reply is drowned out by the water, but I'm pretty sure he agrees with me. He keeps talking, but I can't understand any of it, so I finish applying some makeup, not bothering with much since it's just Cassie. Then I run some product through my wet hair so it air dries nicely.

I'm just giving myself a once-over in the mirror—how Jackie lives without a full-length mirror is beyond me—when Philip steps out of the shower. He whistles and reaches out for me, but I evade his grasp, tossing a towel over his head.

"Aw, no fair, babe," he whines, toweling his wet hair off. As always, the curls stick out every which way, but he doesn't seem to care.

I peer at him, then my hair products. "Can I try something?"

"Does it involve more sex?" He waggles his eyebrows, taking a slow step closer.

Laughing, I grab a tube off the counter. "It doesn't. At least, not right now. But it might get you laid later." I wink, then flip open the cap, squeezing a dollop of product out onto my fingers.

I finger comb his hair, separating and defining the curls on top, squeezing as much water out as I can. He'd never have the patience to let me do a proper routine on his hair, but I've always wondered what it would look like if it was at least a little bit styled.

"You're too tall," I grouse, pushing his shoulders until he kneels on the bathroom mat.

"Not a complaint I've ever heard before, but sure, babe. Whatever you say." As he continues his running commentary of how I'm pulling his hair out, his fingers brush the backs of my knees. I jerk, but he doesn't let go, sliding his hands up the back of my thighs.

His touch is so light that it tickles at the same time it sends a wave of need through me. "Stop that." I twitch as his wandering fingers trace the curve of my ass.

Philip groans. "I'm going to be thinking about how your ass feels in my hands all afternoon. How perfectly round it is and how much I want to bury my face in your pussy."

My cheeks, the ones on my face, go hot at his words. I shouldn't be surprised that he's so vocal about what he wants—the man never stops talking—but to hear him talk about me and my body that way takes me by surprise every time.

Laughing to hide my embarrassment, I keep twisting and arranging the curls around his face as he explores under my dress, not making eye contact. He keeps up a litany of the things he's going to imagine while he's working, including laying me out on the bar top and eating me out, and pressing me up against the wall of windows and taking me from behind while we watch the sunset over the fields. Each scenario he paints builds a little more pressure inside me. Now I'm going to be thinking about them all afternoon too.

"Ophie, you're squirming." His voice is rough as his thumb skates past the apex of my thighs. I jerk my hips, but he has such a firm grip on me that I can't escape. "Are you okay?" He looks up at me with a wicked grin.

"I'm fine," I manage to say through gritted teeth, fighting not to whimper. "Quit teasing me." I push against his forehead as he moves to lift the fabric. "And don't you dare mess up your hair by trying to get under my dress."

Escaping, I turn to grab a small towel so I can squeeze some more water out of his hair.

"Ophelia Moore, will you please..." Philip pauses until I turn to look. He's shifted, bringing one foot out so he's on one knee, a tube of product in his hands. "Share your hair care products with me? Forever?"

The silly gesture makes me laugh, breaking the sexual tension that had been building in the small space. "You idiot." I shake my head. "I'll buy you your own. My hair's not as curly as yours."

"Then will you teach me how to do whatever you just did?" Pushing to his feet, he glances sideways in the bathroom mirror. "I didn't know my hair could look this good."

He turns back to me, hunching his shoulders in a terrible imitation of a model, lips pursed and eyes crossed. Laughing, I push him out the door. "Go work or something. I need to finish getting dressed."

Waggling his eyebrows, he walks away, his whistling echoing back through the cabin as he leaves.

I keep chuckling to myself while I finish my makeup and mess with my own hair before I go meet Cassie. I need the moment alone to remind myself that she can't know about us. And that there is no "us." It's just sex.

Sex with a man who makes me feel safe and seen.

No big deal.

I know I should tell him about the potential job with Zimmerman, but now isn't the time. Either I can surprise him with the good news, or he'll never need to know about yet another failed job lead. I'm sure he's done plenty of interviews while I'm at work that he hasn't told me about for the same reason. We only tell each other *almost* everything. But this is fine. No big deal in the grand scheme of things, since we're both applying to as many jobs as possible.

Pushing it from my mind, I finish getting ready and wander up to the tasting room.

By the time Cassie strolls in, I'm waiting for her with a chilled bottle of riesling and two glasses in hand. I've been eyeing a table in the far corner of the outside patio, praying that no one else takes it. It just happens to be as far away from the bar, and Philip, as possible.

Ophie

I BARELY PAY ATTENTION to Cassie's story about TJ's sunburn. The yellow jacket that's been hovering near her for the last twenty minutes has landed on a curl of her hair, and I can't decide if I should tell her, flick it off myself, or wait and see if it flies off on its own.

I've seen what Cassie does around regular bees, so I can only imagine the flailing and shouting that will happen if I say something. As long as the little fucker doesn't get any closer to her neck, I'll leave it.

"Ophie? Are you even listening?"

I pull my eyes away from the black-and-yellow insect. "You were telling me about the giant piece of skin you peeled off TJ's back, and I was thinking about how utterly disgusting that is."

"Oh god, it was soooooo satisfying." Cassie giggles before finishing off her glass of wine. "This is so good. Why haven't we come here more often?"

"Because we were too busy trying to graduate?" I take another sip from my glass, enjoying the crisp, high-acid flavor. "Us poor grad students had neither the time nor money to come to a place like this."

The wasp zips from Cassie's hair to the table, landing once again on the empty charcuterie platter sitting on the table between us. She doesn't seem to notice it as it crawls over the edge closest to her.

"Some of us are still technically too poor to come to this kind of place." My tone is sharper than necessary as I swirl my glass, the half inch of wine left inside barely moving. If job applications were still on paper, I'd have leveled a forest with the number I've filled out. "Not all of us had a job waiting for us as soon as we graduated."

I look up to see a hurt expression on my friend's face. "Shit, I'm sorry, Cass. I didn't mean it, I promise. I'm just frustrated with the job search, that's all."

Giving me grace, she pats my hand. "I know. It was just luck, really, that my internship last summer turned out so well." She picks up her glass to take a drink, then sets it down again when she sees that it's empty. "Still no luck?"

"I actually have an interview tomorrow with a place that seems really interesting, except that it's on the East Coast." I tell her the rest, including some background on Penny Zimmerman.

"What's wrong with that? You don't have anything keeping you here in Portland, not really." Cassie shrugs, slapping her hand down on the table, mere inches from the damned yellow jacket.

"Yeah, but my whole family is here." I glance around, trying not to look in Philip's direction. "My life is here."

Cassie rolls her eyes. "Be for real, Ophie. It's a great opportunity. Besides, you haven't even done the interview yet. Why are you saying no before you even know if you like the woman or not?"

"But—"

"I'm just saying, don't write off an opportunity like that just because you don't like change."

The yellow jacket, which had been busy making sure the platter was truly empty, changes direction, taking off from the plate and flying right at my face.

I squeak and twist in my seat, hoping it'll fly past me, but the wasp lands right on my chest. Now it's my turn to avoid reacting as its tiny legs tickle my skin. Cassie is shouting at me not to move, but all I want to do is flick it off me. Another voice, a man's, calls out, but I don't listen. All my attention is on the fucking bug that is making its way toward my cleavage. I'm generally a "live and let live" kind of gal when it comes to bugs, but not when they're trying to get under my shirt.

"Don't move." A large hand reaches toward my chest, and I squeak again. "I'm sorry, ma'am, please don't move." A thick finger reaches even closer, brushing the wasp away from my skin. I'm more surprised by a strange man touching my breasts than the angry wasp buzzing in response.

I jerk, the hand in front of me twitches, and the yellow jacket flies angrily in my face all at once. "Pork 'n beans, that smarts. Ma'am, hold still and I'll get it."

"How am I supposed to hold still when there is a very angry wasp inches from my face?" My words come out stilted, my eyes crossing while I try to keep an eye on the insect. "Are these guys the ones that will call their buddies?"

"Don't move, Ophie!" Cassie sounds far away, like she ran from the table. Which is exactly what I expect happened.

The yellow jacket is still buzzing in my face, darting from my ear to my chin, then up to my hairline. I attempt to track it with my eyes while focusing on breathing through my nose and holding still. Unfortunately, there's nothing I can do to stop the scared whine that Cassie keeps making. There's an electric *bzzzt* noise, and then the scent of burning fills my nose.

"Ma'am, it's safe now." The pleasant southern drawl belongs to the man standing in front of me. He's tall, with a polo shirt tucked neatly into a pair of tan slacks. Arrestingly bright blue eyes stare out at me from under dark brows and perfectly swooped hair.

"Oh my god, what is that thing? It's so cool." Cassie reaches out to take what looks like a metal tennis racket from him.

He hands it over without looking at her. "It's a bug zapper. Ma'am, are you alright? Did it get you? Are you allergic to bee stings?"

Cassie shakes the dead insect out of the zapper before waving it around like she's playing tennis with an invisible opponent. My heart is pounding so fast that I'm a little nauseated, but I shake my head at the polite stranger as I catch my breath. "I'm fine. Thank you for zapping it with your racket thingy."

"I'm Cassie, by the way," she pipes up as there's another *bzzzt*. "Yes! Got him. The cutie you just saved from imminent pain is Ophelia. I'm married. She's single." Cassie adds the last bit without a shred of self-consciousness, even though my cheeks burn hot.

What a wingwoman. Not only is she telling the man who just touched my boob my name, but did she have to add that I'm single?

"Well, mighty nice to meet you, Mrs. Cassie. Ms. Ophelia." He tips an invisible hat in our direction, emphasizing his good-ole-boy charm with an exaggerated "Ms."

"Just Ophelia is fine." I try to squash down my irritation at the situation. The man is being polite; it's highly unlikely he's trying a line on me right now. *I* know I could have handled the situation fine, but he couldn't have.

"My mama would have my hide if I didn't mind my manners." He tips his chin and winks, before taking my hand and kissing the back of it. "Jaxon Jones, at your service."

Strangely, the more he tries to be charming, the less I like him. His drawl and hat-tipping feel like an act. When Philip does it, I know he means it, even when he's being goofy. I pull my hand free and lean back in my chair.

Cassie, however, doesn't seem to feel the same way. "Goodness, I don't think we've ever met a real southern gentleman." Her terrible fake drawl makes me cringe, but since she hasn't taken her eyes off him and he's busy kissing the back of her hand—not the one with the deadly tennis racket—my eye roll goes unnoticed.

"Well, I'm just happy I was here in the right place at the right time. How are you enjoying this fine establishment?" He waves a hand at the sloping hill below us.

"Oh, we love this place. We come here all the time." A slight exaggeration in her case. "Ophie's sister is getting married to one of the guys who works here."

"Ah, so you're regular patrons?" He turns to me, eyes dropping to my chest and back up, almost too quickly to notice. "And congratulations to your sister. Love is a fine thing, isn't it?"

"Thank you," I murmur. I grab my glass, forgetting it's empty until I try to take a drink. Well, fuck.

Jaxon indicates the large party at a nearby table, then starts describing his relationship to each. I lose count around the fourth cousin twice removed and start debating with myself over how rude it would be to go get another bottle from Philip.

"And where is your husband, Mrs. Cassie?"

"At home. We just got back from our honeymoon, and I needed a break from his face." Cassie laughs. "Since Ophie is out here hiding from her sister's sex noises—"

"Cassie!" My ears burn as I swat at my friend. "Don't talk about that."

But Jaxon joins her laughter, pausing to give me a knowing look. A look that says he might be interested in learning more about these sex noises, and I wonder if he's really as much of a gentleman as he claims. Where is Philip when I need him?

Except that Cassie is here, and she doesn't know about us, so he can't just swoop in and stake his claim on me with a kiss like he did at the restaurant.

Cassie huffs when I don't join in on the amusement. "Ugh, fine. It was funny, though. Anyway"—she turns back to Jaxon—"we are having a girls' day and catching up since we haven't seen each other in a few weeks. No husbands allowed."

Just as she says it, *my* husband walks up to the table.

"Are you girls alright?" Philip's accent is music to my ears after Jaxon's languid drawl. "I heard yelling?"

"You heard yelling and stopped to grab a bottle of wine?" Jaxon's drawl slips a little, his tone clipped at the end.

"Right, well, it stopped, and when I looked through the window, everyone seemed to be okay, so I paused to bring reinforcements." He hefts the bottle of red in his hand. "I grabbed one of the library pinots from the back."

"Philip, this is Jaxon Jones. There was a yellow jacket buzzing in my face, and he very kindly killed it for us." I step in. "Jaxon, this is my best friend, Philip."

Jaxon doesn't look convinced, angling his body between us. "I saw you inside earlier, didn't I?"

"Sure did, mate. You sure you're okay, Ophie?" Philip moves around him, his eyes glued to me as he comes to stand beside my chair.

"Yeah, I'm fine. It was just a bee—"

"And Jaxon saved her from being stung," Cassie interrupts, a little too gleefully, as Philip leans between me and Jaxon, setting the wine bottle on the table.

He straightens, turning to face Jaxon, his back to me. "You saved her...from a bee?" His shoulder twitches, and the fist that's clenched on his hip opens up to waggle fingers at me.

And just like that, I know he's remembering last summer when he was the one freaking out over a bee, and I was the one who called him a ninny and killed it with my shoe.

Philip is extremely allergic to bees, a fact I learned when he panicked over the wasp nest Maggie discovered inside a planter she'd picked up on Facebook marketplace.

I reach out to tug on the back of his shirt, the linen fabric soft under my fingers. He turns to look at me before moving back a few steps and draping his arm over my shoulder. "Don't worry, it's dead. Actually, we should get one of those bug zappers for you, babe."

The term of endearment drops from my lips so naturally that it takes me an embarrassingly long time to figure out that's why Cassie's jaw is on the floor and Jaxon is eyeing us suspiciously.

Jaxon clears his throat and steps back. "Well, I think that's my cue to exit stage left, pursued by a bear." His southern drawl is completely gone as he scampers back to the table on the other side of the patio.

"What the fuck was that all about?" Cassie's voice is incredulous.

"Was he faking that accent the whole time?" Philip asks, his fingers rubbing a soothing circle on my upper arm.

"Who cares about him. What's happening here?" She drops into her seat, pointing from Philip to me and back. "I've seen you do the fake-dating act before, but she's *never* called you babe before. It's always 'shnookums' or 'boo-bear,' or something equally nauseating."

Shit. I got too comfortable. I force myself to shrug and pull away from Philip. "Nothing happening here. Just fending off yet another douche canoe."

Cassie glares at us for a second, then reaches for the bottle he brought out. "What's this?"

He takes the change of topic and reaches for the bottle, popping the cork out and filling our glasses. "Nate pulled this out earlier so I could try it, and the bottle was still out. Apparently, they only have a dozen left. They bottled these when he and Kel graduated from high school. See the sticker on the back?"

His hand drops to the back of my chair as he straightens, his thumb brushing the back of my neck. I want to close my eyes and purr like a cat at the sensation, especially with the sun shining on my shoulders.

Instead, I take the bottle he's offering and burst out laughing. The usual back-of-the-bottle label has been replaced with a black-and-white picture of two small boys. They're wearing matching overalls and rain boots, their faces covered in streaks of mud as they hold up handfuls of grape bunches. Young Kel's face is split with a wide grin, his light hair sticking up in all directions. I've seen that grin in the months since he and Maggie got together.

But baby Nate? He's like a different person in this picture. There's no trace of the angry asshole who stomps around the winery these days. The picture shows a carefree kid caught in the act of laughing, his open mouth full of half-chewed grapes. There's a fuzzy bit in the corner, and as I peer closer, I make out the top of a head, most likely Sydney's.

How sad that they cut her out of the photo, but I suppose it makes sense if this was for Nate and Kel's graduation.

"Don't try and get out of it—something is up with you two." My feisty friend snatches the bottle from me to look at the photo.

"Cassie, there's nothing going on," I insist, sitting up straighter so that Philip's thumb falls away from my skin, mourning the loss even as I do it.

He holds both hands up in a show of innocence. "Nothing going."

She tips her head to the side, one eyebrow raised, staring at us for a long moment before picking up her wine glass and taking a slow sip. I relax as she seems to switch her focus to it instead of me. Until she sets the glass down and spears Philip with a look. "Did Ophie tell you about her interview tomorrow for the job on the East Coast?"

"Yup, it's a great opportunity," he lies, a little too brightly. "I gotta go, I can see folks walking up." With that, he's gone.

Shit, shit, shit. He's upset; I can tell from the way he didn't look at me before leaving. Why didn't I tell him about it earlier? Guilt gnaws at my stomach, competing with the adrenaline from earlier to make me queasy.

Cassie peers at me over the rim of her glass. "See, Philip agrees with me. You gotta at least try, Ophie. Even if it goes nowhere, it's an amazing opportunity. Who cares if it's not here? Now is the time to try, before you settle down with someone." The abrupt change of subject is welcome, even if thinking about moving across the country and leaving everyone I know behind terrifies me.

She doesn't give me a chance to answer before continuing, apparently oblivious to my distress. "Wasn't that your whole deal, anyway? The reason you and Philip never dated anyone. So that you could graduate and then pursue whatever opportunity came your way without worrying about a significant other?"

Silence stretches on for an uncomfortable minute while she takes a sip.

I stall by sipping my own wine and concentrating on the flavor. The deep red is full-bodied, the fruit notes powerfully hitting the back of my throat, but smooth from being bottled for so long.

"How long have you two been banging?"

The sip of wine in my mouth threatens to go down the wrong tube, and I almost spit it out. Cassie merely sits there across from me, sipping her wine and smirking while I struggle. When I finally catch my breath, she sets her glass down and folds her hands in front of her.

"We're—"

"Before Vegas?"

"We're not—"

"Don't lie to me, Ophelia. You're terrible at it."

I don't try to argue because she's right. I am a terrible liar, and I know she would see right through me.

She tips her head again. "Has to have been recent. I don't think you could have hidden this from me for that long. Look at you—I've never seen you turn this red. Not even when you got sunburned that time we went to the coast."

I cross my arms and look away, my ears burning even as I deny it. "I'm red because it's fucking hot out here, Cassie."

"You didn't give that southern-fried piece of ass a second glance, but the second Philip came outside, you couldn't look away."

"He's my best friend." The argument is so old it tastes stale in my mouth, even if it's still true. Philip is still my best friend. It's just that he's also more.

"Jaxon was practically offering you a roll in the hay—or vines—on a silver platter." Her hair shines in the bright sunlight as she shakes her head. "Jesus, Ophie. You didn't even glance at his ass. And it was a fine-looking specimen."

"Cassie!" I jump at the chance to change the subject. "What about TJ?"

"What about him? He would agree with me." She waves away my protest. "I'm married, not dead. Besides, I've seen you check out plenty of other guys before. And Jaxon, fake drawl or not, was *hot*. And Philip is cute in a *Great British Baking Show* kind of way, not hot in a *Love Island* kind of way."

"You're ridiculous."

"I'm right." Cassie smirks.

The more I argue with her, the more she's going to dig. Besides, I'm tired of keeping this a secret when all I really want is to twirl through the grass like a love-sick puppy. I throw my hands up in the air with a groan. "Okay, fine." I lean my elbows on the table and drop my voice to a whisper. "Yes. We had sex."

"I knew it!" Cassie fist pumps, then leans her elbows on the table to match me, nearly knocking over her glass. "I have so many questions. Since when? How was it? Are you, like, together for reals now? How could you keep something so momentous from me?"

She stops with a deep breath, but all her questions open up a pit of dread in my stomach that replaces the momentary relief of telling her. This is exactly why I didn't want to tell anyone. Because I would have to explain so much—and then explain all over again when Philip leaves and we break things off.

I take a deep breath and tick the answers off on my fingers. "A few days after graduation. It was amazing. And no, we're not together. It's just sex. Nothing more."

The lie hurts my stomach, but if I keep telling myself it doesn't mean anything, maybe I'll start to believe it.

Philip

NATE GRUNTS AS I hand him another case. "So, what's up with you and the sister?"

His question is so unexpected that I almost drop the case of wine I'd just picked up. "Excuse me?"

"You and Maggie's sister. What's the deal?" He hefts another case and adds it to the stack.

The tasting room closed thirty minutes ago. Cassie left an hour ago, a knowing look on her face when she hugged me goodbye. I have a feeling she knows something she shouldn't, but I wasn't going to ask, when not only Nate but also a cluster of customers were standing nearby.

Besides, I have my own questions for my wife. Like what Cassie meant by an opportunity on the East Coast? Why don't I know anything about this?

"She's a good friend. My best friend," I finally answer, moving to the next stack he brought in from storage.

Ole When-we pauses, his hands digging into the small of his back as he arches his spine. "Your best friend often sleeps over? And wears your shirt while drinking coffee on the front porch?"

I make a sound of protest, but he keeps talking.

"It's real quiet out here at night. Sound carries."

The heavy case slips as I set it on the floor, pinching my finger. "Fuck." I step back, shaking it off. The storage room at the back of the wine bar is just big enough for the pair of us to move around in, but not enough that I can pace off the pain. I back out of the room, Nate taking over the stack I was moving.

I'd been ready to race down to my cabin and see Ophie when he'd appeared at the back door, a dolly stacked with cases. After helping him wheel up another six stacks from the cellar beneath the main building, I'd felt obligated to stay and help him organize the upstairs storage.

"Hurts like a bitch, right?" Nate's leaning against the doorframe, arms crossed. "I saw a guy in Bordeaux get his whole hand crushed. It got caught under a dolly when we were packaging cases."

"Damn. That sounds awful." I shake my hand out again, the pain receding. "And, um...sorry? For the noise, I mean."

"Better than hearing Kel and Maggie. Listening to your best friend have sex should be illegal." He smirks as I hand him another case. "Unless you're also participating, I guess."

I burst out laughing. "You got me there, mate."

I've never seen Nate this relaxed, but if he's going to remove an inch of stick from his ass, I'll take the mile. "How's the growing going? Not sure what the right word is, but you know what I mean."

"Crop is looking good so far, although I hope we don't get too many more heat waves this summer. The pinots don't tolerate the heat so well."

We keep stacking and sorting the bottles as he waxes on about different grape varieties he wants to try that might do better with the changing climate. He's downright chatty, like he hasn't had a real conversation in months and has been bottling it all up with no one to talk to.

"How many people are you expecting at the wine club event this weekend? If you need some extra help, I could see if Ophie is free? She works at Latte Da, so she knows how to serve and work a crowd."

In truth, I just want an excuse to keep her here a little longer. I missed waking up to the sound of her singing in the shower, or her arm being thrown across my chest in her sleep. I just miss her.

"Are you going to work or flirt?"

"We would be the utmost professionals." I pause, shoving a couple of bottles deeper onto a shelf with a grunt. "Besides, it's kind of a secret? And Maggie would be there..."

"Ah. I see." Nate does that old-fashioned nose touch thing that I've never understood. "If she's free, I'm sure we could use the help. Anything to keep the Sutton girl from being a nuisance. She's hell-bent on working here, and I don't know how much longer I can hold her off."

Grabbing more bottles, I keep stacking them on the shelves. "Emma? Why are you so against her helping out? She seems eager enough, and she wouldn't drive away customers with a grumpy attitude."

"Touché." Nate laughs. It's the first time I've ever heard him sound so human. "For starters, she's not twenty-one yet, and she'd have to take a test and get a pourer's permit, which we don't have time for before Saturday. But most importantly, Sophie Sutton made me promise not to let her work here. Not until she graduates."

He shakes his head, grunting as he stacks more wine. "I may not like the Suttons or the fact that they bought my home, but I'm not stupid enough to piss off Sophie. Especially when it comes to her kid."

The last box unloaded, I follow Nate out of the storage room so he can lock up. He pockets his keys and starts off toward his cabin. I'm just a few steps behind when he turns around. "I'm going to shower and then head into town for a drink. Probably be gone for a couple hours. Hopefully, I can get a good night's sleep tonight."

He turns and is gone before I can answer, leaving me at the top of the path leading down to the cabins. I'm still chuckling as I open the front door. Ophie is sitting on the couch, her feet tucked up underneath her dress, laptop on her knees. Her hair is pulled up off her neck with a clip, one long strand that she must have missed trailing down her neck.

A hint of sweat dots her temples from the hot day, and her cheeks are flushed. The flush deepens when she looks up and sees me.

"Cassie knows—"

"Nate definitely knows—"

We both speak at the same time, choking off the words. "You told Cassie?"

Ophie sets her laptop on the coffee table, hugging her knees. "She guessed. Apparently, I need to work on my poker face."

"So, what did you tell her?" I perch on the cushion beside her, letting my hand cover hers. When she's silent for a moment, I flip her top hand over and lace my fingers with hers, my thumb tracing circles against her skin. "Ophie?"

"Nothing, really."

I lift her hand and kiss it, my tongue slipping out to taste her skin. "Did you tell her it was the best sex of your life?"

A delicious grin tips her lips. "I told her it was amazing, yeah."

I pull her closer, tucking our joined hands between my legs, her knees coming down on the couch beside my thigh as she resettles beside me. "Did you tell her we broke the bed?"

I pull her close and kiss her cheek, then her jaw.

She lets out a quiet sigh before answering. "No."

"Why not?" I keep kissing along her jaw, dotting extra kisses in the space beneath her chin just for fun.

Her ears turn as pink as the rest of her skin, and she pulls as far away as she can. "Because it's embarrassing?"

"It's embarrassing that I flipped you over my shoulder?" I loosen one hand and slide it between her ass and her calves, threatening to pick her up and flip her over me. She squeaks and sits down hard, trapping my arm.

Fortunately for me, this position has her collarbones and breasts at the perfect height for my lips and tongue to explore. Especially with the delightful way her dress plunges low, inviting me in.

"Philip," she whispers but doesn't pull away. "It's embarrassing that we had sex while Sydney was passed out drunk in the other room."

My arms and legs slacken with surprise at her point of view, and she pulls free. "One, she was not passed out drunk, she was just sleepy drunk." Ophie snorts at my perspective but doesn't argue. "And two, I just can't resist you. No one on earth could possibly have enough willpower to walk away from you."

"That's bullshit. People walk away from me all the time." Just like she's willing to walk away from me, apparently. She snorts and tries to pull away, but I catch her before she can get far, this time pulling her across my lap before capturing her lips in a deep kiss.

"If they walk away from you, then they don't matter, liefling." I kiss her again. "But most importantly, *I* couldn't walk away from you. Not when everything between us was so new." I feel like there's more to uncover here, but her lips and body are too much temptation for me to resist.

So we stop talking and start kissing. A good old-fashioned make-out session with Ophie draped across me, her ass nestled between my thighs.

The kind that used to get me in trouble with the girls at school as a teenager. Well, the girls didn't seem to mind—it was their brothers who objected when I didn't follow up the making out with a declaration of everlasting love.

Tonight, it's working to distract me from all the questions we're carefully not asking. Or answering.

My fingers are already working their way underneath Ophie's dress, and I can feel her heat ready to welcome me. She squirms, rubbing my dick just right through my jeans. "Yes," she breathes, throwing her head back as my fingers skate across her underwear, already damp.

Unable to resist teasing, I slide my fingers beneath the edge of her panties, barely grazing her lower lips. I brace and lift her close enough to whisper in her ear. "And did you tell her that you're madly in love with me?"

Ophie opens one eye, barely turning her head to look at me, and smirks. "I told her the truth—"

My heart races at her words. The truth? The real truth? That we got married on a whim, and there's a possibility that maybe we've been in love this whole time?

She bites my ear, swirling her tongue against the sensitive nerves there, before whispering, "I told her that we were just banging."

I didn't think my heart could break at the same time my dick could get hard. I thought men weren't good at multitasking.

My breath escapes in a low moan, half from the sensation of her lips against my skin and half from sadness. But I force myself not to react, not to correct or contradict her. It doesn't matter that my feelings are deeper, that I want more.

This was the reminder I needed that Ophie doesn't want a romantic relationship with me. And I don't want to lose her. Losing her would leave me anchorless, adrift in a sea of choices with no idea which way to turn.

So I push aside my feelings and concentrate on the feel of her wet heat and the way my stroking fingers make her moan. She kisses me again, our tongues dancing as our mouths meet. I keep stroking her, two digits slipping inside while my thumb finds her clit.

Mouths still fused, she vibrates with pleasure against my lips. My thumb continues circling as her humming gets higher pitched and her back stiffens.

With an inarticulate cry, she pulls back, her nails digging into my shoulders as she falls apart. There's a faint contraction around my fingers and her breathing peaks then slows.

"Definitely the best sex of my life," she murmurs before her eyes come back into focus and I pull her dress straight. "Not that I would tell Cassie."

The broken pieces of my poor heart flap sadly inside my chest. I must make some kind of noise because her eyes snap to my face and narrow.

"What's wrong?"

I lean in and capture her lips in a sweet kiss. "Nothing."

As soon as our lips part, Ophie shifts, turning to get a better look at me. "Something's wrong. You have that eye thing."

"What eye thing?" I touch the side of my face. What is she talking about?

She points to the side of her eye. "When you're worried, or there's something you're not telling me, your eyes get tight right here." She moves to touch the side of my face. "It's like squinting but not."

"I'm not doing an eye thing." Relaxing my face is hard, and I don't want to admit that I can feel the tension around my eyes loosen when I make a conscious effort. "And nothing is wrong."

As she wriggles, her sit bones dig painfully into my thighs. "Philip. Are you mad I told Cassie? She guessed. Apparently, I wasn't checking out Jaxon enough. And you know I'm a terrible liar."

"I'm not mad Cassie found out. Nate already knows. And it's not like your sister hasn't almost caught us more than once."

"Then why are you upset?"

"I'm not upset."

She narrows her eyes at me. "You are."

"I'm not." My casual attempt at saying it doesn't fool her. It wouldn't fool anyone. But god, I wish she would let it drop so I don't have to explain why I'm upset.

"So, you'd be happy to just make out with me all night, no conversation required?" Shifting, she swings one leg over my thighs so she's straddling me. But instead of pressing close and letting me go back to pretending all I want is sex, she slides back to my knees and pokes a finger in my chest. "Husband. Talk."

Fuck, she's called my bluff.

I take her hands in mine, stalling while I dig deep for the courage to admit the truth that's been twisting my guts for the last four months.

Ophie rubs her thumbs across the back of my knuckles, the motion soothing, just like always. My gaze is glued to our hands resting on my thighs.

She always knows how to make me feel better. Braver. More myself than the charming vagabond who arrived in America with two suitcases and the knowledge that there was no going back home. She grounds me. Reminds me that there are more important things in this life.

"I don't want to keep lying." I finally find the words to start.

"I mean, I don't like it either, but we agreed—"

"Not to everyone else." I look up, meeting her confused eyes. "To you."

Her hands jerk in mine, but I keep hold. "To me? What are you lying to me about?"

I take a deep breath, bracing myself for some kind of explosion. Good or bad, I'm not sure. "It's not just sex. For me." Ophie doesn't say anything, and I keep babbling, not sure how to stop once the words start. My focus drifts back to our hands as I stumble through my confession.

"I love you. Not just as my best friend. I mean, you *are* my best friend. You'll always be my best friend. But I don't know if that's enough. Not anymore." I turn my head to the side, afraid to see her expression.

"Philip, I—" Ophie chokes off the word and falls silent.

The quiet is broken only by the slam of a car door outside and the rumble of Nate's engine starting.

As my heart slams against my ribcage, Ophie shifts, releasing me as she stands. I let go of her hands, tucking mine between my knees, my shoulders slumping. A moment later, she sits beside me on the couch, right in my line of vision.

Her brown eyes are glassy, a tear threatening to fall from one. Her chin quivers as she parts her lips to take a breath. "You ninny," she whispers, the words broken and catching as she hiccups. "It's not enough for me either."

The rest of her words are cut off as I cup her jaw and pull her in. I need to kiss her again like I need to breathe. In a desert, she's my oasis. The air my lungs burn for after a deep dive. My home. Touching her, tasting her, melting into her—it's not a choice.

Ophie makes a contented noise, kissing me back as fiercely as I'm kissing her. Lightning strikes as her hands slide under my shirt, leaving hot trails against my stomach and chest. Eventually, I pull back with a relieved chuckle.

"I love you, Ophelia." The words are so familiar. I've said them to her a million times before today, but I never meant them like this before. "You are everything to me. My best friend, my better half, the rock who keeps me from drowning."

She opens her mouth, but I keep going, laying my finger across her lips so I can finish. "You are smart. Determined. Gentle and compassionate. Why you put up with my silly ass is beyond me, but I am so thankful that you do. Also, you're hot as hell. Like, definitely out of my league."

"Don't say that—" She smacks lightly at my arm.

I grin, but I'm right and she knows it. "Mrs. van der Merwe, I love you. Can we please make this marriage real?"

Ophie

FOR THE FIRST TIME since Vegas, being called Mrs. van der Merwe makes my stomach swoop in a good way. Philip's confession has been slowly melting me from the inside out. At this point, the only thing holding me together might be my skin, and even that is two seconds away from melting off me.

"Are you asking me to date you? Like, officially?" I have to ask. We've been so nebulous for so long that all I want right now is clarity.

Philip grabs me by the hips and pulls me over his lap again so we're eye to eye. "No, Ophelia. We've been 'dating' for two years. I want to be married to you. Forever. With everything that comes with it."

I stare into his eyes for a long minute and find nothing but the truth. There's no hint of uncertainty. There's no sign of the crooked wrinkle between his eyebrows that only appears when he's unsure of something. There's just Philip, looking at me like he's never going to stop.

I know we still need to talk about what comes next. Would he be willing to come to South Carolina with me? Would I be willing to go to Australia or anywhere else in the world with him? Guilt bites at the back of my mind, reminding me I haven't even told him about my interview with Penny tomorrow. But right now, I don't care. Right now, all I want is to bask in the certainty that we love each other.

Everything else is just details.

I lean forward and press a kiss to his lips. "I'm in."

With a whoop, Philip scoops me up and carries me to the bedroom. My dress hits the floor somewhere on the way, his shirt and jeans not far behind. In moments, I'm lying on my back on the bed, staring up at my husband as he climbs over me.

"My liefling," he whispers into my skin, his lips trailing along my stomach.

"What does that mean?" I push up to my elbows, watching as he nears my pussy. "You promised to tell me."

He hooks his thumbs in the sides of my underwear, inching them down my thighs. "It means 'my darling.'"

All the times he's said it over the years, I always assumed it was a reference to my being short. Or my not-so-secret love of fantasy books. "That's what you've been calling me all this time?"

"Are you upset?" His eyes are glued to mine as he starts kissing up the inside of my leg. The sensation is featherlight but rockets straight to my core, stoking the embers of desire that have been burning there all damn day.

"It's very hard to be anything other than a mushy pile of need right now."

Pain and pleasure chase up my spine as he nips the sensitive skin of my inner thigh. "Good. That's how I like you best."

He works his way closer to my aching core and I writhe. "Phil-ip." It comes out with a half whine, half moan as he hooks my leg over his shoulder, his thumbs opening me while he gazes at me.

"I wasn't sure I'd ever get to learn this most secret part of you, Ophie. I need to study it—I haven't had as long to learn my way around your pretty pussy." Before I can object, he dives in, his tongue delving between my labia, mapping every centimeter of me.

The tingling of pleasure that had been building surges through me as he continues to explore. The intensity is different this time. He's not tentative like the first time or slightly detached like before. This time, he eats me out like he owns me, like my body is his to enjoy. He's not wrong.

When he finally comes up for air, and I'm a panting mess, he grins at me over the edge of my body. "The first time you moaned my name...I knew I never wanted to hear anyone else say it again."

It's my turn to claim him, and I do. I roll him under me, straddling his hips and guiding him inside me. The moment his cock fills me is like putting the final piece in a puzzle—the whole picture becomes clear. "I love you," I say over and over again as I ride him.

I crest that wave again, another orgasm washing over me as my hips jerk and my fingers grip his chest. Without waiting for me to finish coming, Philip rolls us over, thrusting into me and whispering the words right back.

He keeps the same steady pace, arms caging me in as he makes love to me. "Liefling," he whispers over and over in my ear, his lips trailing kisses along my jaw and neck.

Another orgasm builds on top of the last, and I wrap my heels around his calves, pulling him deeper with each thrust. "Almost there," I grunt, shifting my hips to find friction as we move together.

With a groan, Philip pushes up on one hand, using the leverage to scrape my clit with each thrust. His back stiffens as he calls my name one more time, still thrusting as his orgasm pumps into me until I also come apart once more.

Later, golden light drapes across Philip's shoulders as we lie spent on the bed. The setting sun paints the skin on his back an even deeper tan than normal. Head resting on his arms, Philip faces me, his eyes closed against the bright light streaming through the window.

"I'm not dreaming this, right? This is really real?"

"Yes, it's real." I push up to press a kiss to his shoulder blade. "But now we have to figure out what to tell everyone."

This is the part I've been most afraid of. As if he senses the anxiety bubbling up inside me, he reaches over and pulls me against his chest, spooning me from behind.

"What are you afraid of?"

"That this is going to change everything. What if my family thinks it's a terrible idea?" My words are a whisper, barely audible. "But I can't bear the thought of losing you. Why does everything have to keep changing on me?"

He squeezes me from behind, pressing a kiss behind my ear. "I hate to break it to you, Ophelia, but you were the one who made everything change. No take-backsies."

"But—"

He cuts me off, turning my face back to capture my lips. "*You* were the one who suggested getting married 'just in case.'"

"I saw you looking at flights to Australia. I panicked."

Philip chuckles, the rumble of his chest vibrating against my back. "*You* were the one who came home from work and walked naked into my room." His fingertips trail over my side, lighting my skin on fire.

I squirm, thighs rubbing together to relieve the ache building between them. "You started it." He was the one who kissed me in the restaurant, making me question everything I'd ever assumed about how he felt.

The one whose accidental kiss left me feeling empowered. I wasn't the one who changed everything. He was.

Except maybe I was. Maybe every time there was a hint that he might drift away, I'd held on tighter. Given him another reason to stay.

"By spitting toothpaste in your face? I didn't realize you were into that kind of kink." He chuckles as he presses open-mouth kisses along the back of my neck.

"No, when you kissed me in the restaurant. I couldn't stop thinking about what it meant."

Philip chuckles again. "After you loudly claimed me as your husband."

I open my mouth to argue, but he cuts me off.

"But maybe I did push it a bit." He trails his lips and tongue along my naked shoulder. "Maybe I took advantage of the situation to see what you would do if I nudged us over the line."

I lie there while he peppers kisses along my shoulder and back. If I'm really the one who started it all, who took the first step over the line toward this moment, then Philip has matched me step for step. And so what? All the energy I've spent worrying about keeping things the same, and never once did I see that I was the one who kept pulling us down the path.

That every decision I made out of my fear of losing him and our status quo tangled our lives together even more.

"Even if it is all my fault." I finally break the silence. "What happens now?"

"We prepare for everyone to give us shit for a week or so, and then they'll be over it. And then we live our life."

"Our life? I like that." When he puts it like that, it feels like maybe I was worried over nothing. But then I snort, imagining how my sisters are going to react. "Maybe more like a month."

Philip's laughter vibrates against my back. "Cassie is going to gloat for at least a year."

We rank how long our friends and family are going to give us a hard time for finally admitting our feelings—his family is going to be the easier of the two by far—before Philip's stomach rumbles so loudly that neither of us can ignore it.

This time, cooking in Jackie and Greg's kitchen fills me with a sense of rightness. As if we're on our honeymoon, not hiding away from my sister and her fiancé.

"So, how are you enjoying your job as a pseudo-sommelier?" I ask, slicing up a cucumber.

Philip looks up from his phone, leaning his elbows on the counter to study me. "Actually, I like it more than I thought. Nate was explaining to me some of the different ways they bring in revenue, and it's pretty interesting."

He tells me about the rootstock they grow and sell but loses me somewhere between the Italian and French grapes that were devastated by something called phylloxera and German blue slate. I nod and let his voice wash over me as I revel in the peace I feel.

The nagging question of what he's thinking is gone. When I look at him now, I don't see a question or a source of anxiety. I see a man who always includes me, who asks for my opinion, who draws me out of my shell and gives me the courage to be myself with more than just him.

No judgment.

No eye rolling when I get excited about a particularly satisfying pivot table.

Someone who enthusiastically jumps on board with whatever I suggest—and asks the same of me.

"We could go anywhere." I interrupt his detailed monologue about how long it takes the grapes to go from vine to cask during harvest.

"...to harvest grapes? Not really, liefling, we have to be between thirty and fifty degrees latitude."

Shaking my head, I scrape the peppers I finished slicing into the salad bowl. "No, silly. I mean that we could go anywhere. You and me. I could get a job in South Carolina—" I almost choke on the guilt that pushes the name out of my mouth. I'll explain while we eat, I promise myself as I cover up my hesitation with more nonsense. "Or you could get a job in—"

"Singapore? Omaha? But what about your family? Your friends?"

"We could visit." I shrug, feigning nonchalance. Ever since Penny emailed me, I haven't stopped thinking about what it would mean to move away from the PNW. "I mean, Singapore is kind of far, but you know what I mean. Besides"—I point at him with the tongs in my hand—"*your* family is on that side of the world. But the point is, if we're going to do this—be really for real married. And a couple. Well, what's to stop us from going somewhere together?"

Philip takes the salad bowl from me and sets it on the table before coming back to grab the cold chicken I'd found in the fridge. "Would you move to Australia? For me?"

I follow and slide into my seat as he sits beside me. "Do you have a job offer there you didn't tell me about?"

The pink in Philip's cheeks gives away the truth. "My dad's firm has been trying to hire me ever since graduation," he admits. "I never told you about it because I wasn't planning to take it."

We serve up our food in silence while I think about what to say. Something tells me that Philip is waiting for me to say something. Something specific, but I can't figure out what.

Is he waiting for me to blow up at him? Logically, I should be mad that he hid this from me, just like he deserves to be angry at me when I tell him about South Carolina, but I have a suspicion that there's more to the story.

Finally, I break the silence. "And you didn't tell me because you knew I would tell you to seriously consider it, didn't you?"

"Well, yeah." He shifts in his seat, making eye contact as he reaches for my hand. Again, there's a pregnant pause, like he's waiting for something, before he continues. "Mostly, I didn't want to leave you." His hand is warm and firm on mine, squeezing with reassurance.

"And it wasn't because you didn't want to make me feel like I'd married you in Vegas for nothing? That I was possibly committing immigration fraud on your behalf, just for you to go and take off for Australia at the first offer of a job?" I flip my hand over to thread my fingers with his, food forgotten.

"Okay, Ryan Reynolds," he jokes, but then turns serious. "Ophie, do you really think I could have left you behind? Who would keep me on the straight and narrow? Besides, I can barely go two hours without talking to you. What would I have done with a seventeen-hour time difference?"

Every word he says heaps coal on the guilt burning in the pit of my stomach. I have to tell him about Penny, but the words are stuck in my throat, so I deflect instead. "Did I tell you I almost asked Maggie to check on you when you first moved down here and I didn't hear from you?" I pull my hand free so I can eat.

"Did I tell you Maggie checked on me anyway? And fed me dinner. Twice. Made me help Olive with her math homework as payment." Philip grins as he spears food onto his fork and shoves it in his mouth.

I laugh, knowing exactly why my sister arranged that. "My sister hates math with a passion. I used to tutor her on the subject when she was in high school."

A thoughtful expression fills his face as he chews. "If she was in high school, wouldn't you have been in junior school?"

"Middle school," I correct him. "Yeah. But I was in accelerated math classes." Truthfully, since she had to repeat Algebra and I was two years ahead of my peers, we were working out of the same textbook. I know she would probably be embarrassed about it, but those years of doing our math homework together, me helping her when she struggled, are some of my best memories of spending time with her.

We let the conversation turn to reminiscing about school as kids—Jono and Philip were apparently much more competitive with each other than I was with either of my sisters—and the heavy topic of where we go from here drops. I need to tell him about Penny Zimmerman, but not tonight. Not when everything is new and it might ruin this perfect start.

Despite the fact that we're house-sitting for practical strangers—I've vowed never to own a single piece of rooster decor after this—being here with Philip feels normal. Better than normal, actually. Because when we move to the couch to continue our binge-rewatch of *Battlestar Galactica* and Philip pulls me into his chest, the tiny voice at the back of my head that used to wonder if there was more to us than I wanted to admit is silent. And I can wrap my arms around his chest and snuggle into his side without second-guessing if it's appropriate or not.

His lips have tasted every square inch of my skin; there's no part of my body that Philip hasn't touched. Doesn't own.

And when we go to bed hours later, I make sure to brand him with my lips in return. Reveling in the freedom to own my husband as surely as he owns me.

Philip

KEL STARES AT NATE'S phone, eyebrows furrowed as he reads the description Nate showed me a few days ago. "You think Sophie will go for it?" He hands back the phone. "Or Sutton?"

Nate grunts. "Sophie will be the easy sell. Theo will be the one who needs convincing. That's what I'm paying him for." He jerks his thumb in my direction.

Kel turns to look at me, hands shoved deep in his pockets. "Is he paying you to crunch numbers or charm Theo into agreeing with him?"

I grin. "Both?"

"I think it's going to be a harder sell than you think. Why are you pushing for a whole new bottling system? Does this mean you're planning on staying?" Kel leads the way into the cellar, picking up various tools sitting on the counter and putting them away in drawers as he passes.

Nate asked me to come with him to do an inspection of the vines this morning, and I agreed since I don't have anything better to do and Ophie went back to her place late last night.

We're finally ready to go public with our relationship, but she didn't want to run the risk of it happening pre-caffeine. I didn't argue, even though watching her drive away reopened a few of the stitches holding my heart back together. I wouldn't say she looked guilty as she said goodbye, but there was definitely something off. Last night, I gave her plenty of opportunities to elaborate on what Cassie said, but she never did, so as of this morning, I'm assuming I heard wrong and there's nothing to worry about.

Hanging out with Nate and Kel this morning is a welcome—albeit strange—distraction from the worry that ate at me while I should have been sleeping.

Oh, how quickly I went from enjoying a good sprawl in my bed to needing Ophie tucked against my chest in order to get a good sleep. It's been blissful with just the two of us in the cabin. Me working with Nate, Ophie working her shifts at the coffee shop, both of us scrolling endlessly through job postings.

Nate sighs and follows him in, and I trail behind, watching the pair of them. It's easy to see the history between them, the easy familiarity with being in each other's space, even as their words are cautious and overly polite at times.

I've hung out with Kel enough times that I know he's not really as grumpy as he can appear—he's guarded, but once you get him talking, he's a genuinely fun guy. And it only takes five seconds of seeing him with his kid and Maggie to know he would do anything for them.

Nate's been harder to get to know, but over the course of the weeks I've been here, he's thawed out with me. He's got a wicked sense of humor that he rarely shows, and he really does know what he's doing around the winery. He just can't seem to stay civil to the customers who come in.

"Am I staying? Who else is going run this place?"

Kel stops tidying the drawer and turns to face us. Well, Nate. I'm forgotten as the two men face off.

"You don't have to be a martyr to this place, Nate. If you don't want to be here, then go. Go back to France if that's what you want. Whatever life you had out there that kept you from coming home for five years is probably still waiting for you." The hurt dripping from Kel's words feeds the tension building in the air around us.

"And if I leave, who runs this place? Sutton?" Nate growls.

"I'm sure they can hire someone to run it." Kel waves away the question.

"And what happens to my parents? To their home? To *my* home? I just walk away and let them deal with it?"

"Isn't that exactly what you did before? You came home, heard the news, picked a fight with Sydney, and then stormed back off to France without so much as a goodbye." Kel grabs a set of pruning shears and makes to walk past Nate.

But he grabs his arm, stopping him from leaving. "Why do you think I have to stay? I owe it to you, and to this place, to be here. I shouldn't have left like I did. I'm sorry I made you deal with the mess I made." His shoulders drop, and he releases Kel's arm. "This place, I know how to fix—"

Kel snorts, and Nate winces.

"Not fix. You did an amazing job taking care of it. But I know what I'm doing here. It's Sydney I don't know how to fix things with."

"Have you tried apologizing? Have you even talked to her since you've been back?"

"She won't listen to anything I have to say. Every time I try to talk to her, she just walks away."

"I don't know what happened between you two, but she's been a mess since you got back. Did you know I had to pick her up…"

I step further back into the shadow of the casks stacked against the wall. I feel like an intruder, being here while they hash it out. When they don't react, I silently move toward the open roll-up door behind me. Their conversation fades as I step out into the sunshine.

The August heat is intense, the sun brutal while we have yet another heat wave. My feet are trapped in the work boots Nate insists I wear when I do anything out in the vineyard with him. I've dropped the sharp pruning shears enough times to not argue, but I still miss the freedom of my thongs.

I pull my phone out of my pocket, half hoping for a text from Ophie even though I know she probably isn't even awake yet. When there isn't anything, I send her a kissy face emoji, then scroll through my emails while I wait.

An email from Jono's company stares back at me. I'd applied months ago, mostly to appease my family, with no intention of following through unless I got kicked out of the States. But the email confirming my interview with them tomorrow morning feels less performative than it did forty-eight hours ago.

But can I really drag Ophie all the way across the world? And do I even want to?

It's taken two years, but the Pacific Northwest has really grown on me. I still hate the winter here, but the summer and Ophie make up for it. Would it be so bad to stay?

Footsteps echo behind me. I shove my phone back in my pocket as Kel claps a hand on my shoulder. "Sorry. We're still working some shit out."

"No worries, man." I shrug. "Is Nate coming?"

"In a second. Sutton called."

Kel and I shoot the shit while waiting for Nate to reappear. He's excited about the baby and the international culinary class he's taking next term. Listening to him talk about the different directions his life has gone, from nursing to handyman to chef, makes me think that maybe Ophie and I don't have to figure it all out right now. We're only twenty-six—we have time to try out different jobs and places to live.

"So, Nate's got you sold on the reusable bottles?" Kel leans against the cellar door, arms crossed over his chest, one leg kicked over the other.

"To be perfectly honest, I don't have skin in the game either way, but he seems keen to make it work. Numbers-wise, it'll take a few years before he sees any kind of return on it, but if he's got Sutton's backing, I think he could make it work."

If Nate's goal was to make this place as profitable as possible, I wouldn't recommend he be on the front lines of the reusable wine bottle movement. But since he doesn't have the pressure of having to increase profit year over year, he can afford to. Nate is convinced that if he can show Sutton how good he is at running Sunshine, he might be able to buy it back from him one day.

I don't think he meant to let that last idea slip, but he was very impassioned—and a little buzzed—when we discussed it the other night.

"So, he's finally seeing the benefit to Sunshine being owned by a billionaire and his wife who don't actually need it to be profitable?" Kel smirks.

"I think he's finally seeing that Sutton may be the answer to modernizing this place," Nate answers for himself, stepping out into the hot morning air. "Between my dad's stubborn refusal to try anything new, and the French abhorrence to *modernité*"—he adds air quotes to drive home his thoughts on the French—"I'm so tired of hearing 'but we've never done it that way' that I might lose my mind. Sunshine Cellars is a nice little winery that will never be anything more unless we invest in being different. I have lots of ideas and no way to test them."

My brother-in-law clears his throat and indicates Nate should lead the way. We follow in silence toward a row of grapes before he speaks up again. "I noticed that's a local company. How did you find them? Are reusable wine bottles a thing in Europe?"

I follow along, acting as more of a pack mule than anything as Nate and Kel expertly check and assess row after row of grape vines. I have no idea what they're looking for, but it's impressive to see the speed at which they flip over leaves and check on bunches, working as a team despite the fight earlier.

Just like Jono and I having a row, then going surfing twenty minutes later. Thinking about my brother sends a pang through my sternum. He would love this place—Nicola too.

The whole morning, Nate explains all the reasons why the new bottles are a good idea. Kel argues his points, but it feels like he's trying to help Nate finesse his argument rather than really change his mind.

I pipe up where I can, mostly on the numbers since that's what Nate asked me to help him with. I'm not sure he'll be able to convince Sutton on the numbers alone—it is a big investment, and it will set profits back by a large margin—but if he can convince Sophie and Theo that it's the sustainable future, he might have a shot.

The tension from earlier has dissipated by the time we finish inspecting the field Nate chose. The sun is fierce and I'm sweating through my T-shirt and wishing for a bandanna or something to keep the sweat out of my eyes.

"I swear, if I have to hear that song one more time, I'm going to lose my fucking mind." Kel has been complaining about the TikTok dances Maggie and Olive keep practicing. My theory is that Maggie is doing it to keep Olive entertained and not glued to the TV, but my expertise was not requested, so I'm keeping my mouth shut.

"Just get them a pair of AirPods to share. The new noise-canceling ones work surprisingly well. They even block out most of the sex noises you all keep making." Nate's solution is a good one. But he has no idea the unexploded bomb he's just dropped in my lap.

Kel turns to me, eyes wide. "Sex noises?" Before I can defend myself, he chuckles. "Well, at least you only have to listen to it every other week."

Nate turns and points at both of us. "I wish. Between you two, I get to listen to it every fucking night of the week."

Shit. Fuck. By the way Kel is turning his glare on me, I've been caught in the chicken coop. My goose is cooked. He's going to go full big-brother-in-law on me, and I am never going to see my sweet wife's face again.

"You're making sex noises. With who?"

I open my mouth to answer, but nothing comes out. The wheels are still turning in his mind, though, because I can see the exact second he puts two and two together.

"Ophelia? But Maggie insisted...no, it can't be." His face grows redder and redder by the second, matching the heat rising in mine, the hot sun not helping us stay any cooler. "Is this where she's been disappearing to when we're there?"

"It's new." I step backward, out of arm's reach of Kel.

"Is it serious? You're not just fucking around with her before you leave, right?"

My eyes are glued to his hands. Currently, they are relaxed and loose by his sides, but I can sense the tension in his shoulders.

Fuck it. Telling him the truth may be the only way out of this without getting a taste of what he dished out to Nate. But maybe I'll leave out the Vegas/green card bit. For now.

"Yes, it's serious. I've always loved her, and I think she's loved me for a long time too. We just didn't want to risk our goals on an unknown while we were in school." I desperately want to get us back into motion, but I have no idea what they were planning to do next. Risking a glance past Kel, I'm alarmed to find the space where Nate was standing is empty.

The shuffle of dirt behind me and the twitch on Kel's face is the only warning I get before my arms are trapped behind me.

"What the fuck, man." I attempt to pull away, but Nate has too good of a hold on me. "Are you serious right now?"

"Bro code. You mess with my best friend's sister, you gotta be willing to face the consequences." Nate says this without a hint of irony, until Kel rolls his eyes and sighs. "We're not talking about me right now."

"You better be glad we're not," Kel growls before turning his attention back to me.

Relaxing my arms in an attempt to get some leverage, I try reasoning with Kel again. "You realize that Ophie and I are both adults? That she is perfectly capable of making this kind of decision on her own?"

"But she's my future wife's little sister." He shrugs as if that explains everything. "Gotta make sure you have honorable intentions."

I snort. "At least I didn't knock her up before I married her."

Nate releases my arms so fast, I stumble forward, straight into a stunned Kel. Since my ability to breathe is now being threatened by both men, and if either of them tells Maggie before I have a chance to warn Ophie, I take advantage of their shock to book it back to my cabin, pulling my phone out as I run.

She doesn't answer. Kel and Nate's raised voices are still behind me, so I dash inside to grab my keys and hop in my car.

The last thing I hear before the gravel underneath my tires drowns him out is Kel shouting, "What do you mean you married her?"

Ophie

I MANAGE TO HOLD it together through the whole interview despite my phone blowing up with texts and phone calls.

Instead of checking to see what's happening, I leave it facedown on the table beside my laptop and push my chair back to stand. The last hour was so amazing—talking to Penny about her vision and how I could fit into it—I just want to take a moment to enjoy the feeling before I find out what the fuss is about.

Or break the news to Philip that Penny offered me the job on the spot.

I never knew I could feel elated and terrified at the same time. What would it mean for us? Sure, we talked about the hypothetical of one of us getting a job far away, but I never imagined that it would be a real possibility. I never really thought he would leave me. Or I would leave him.

"Ophie?" Philip calls out as I pull out my secret stash of chocolate from the back of the pantry.

"In here." I grab a couple of chocolates, then shove the bag of mini Snickers back behind the canned peas I have no intention of ever eating, and turn. Philip rushes into the kitchen, sweaty and stressed. All thoughts of chocolate and new job opportunities vanish at the worried look on his face.

"What's wrong? What happened?" Maggie's name on the string of texts that caught my eye before I flipped my phone over to concentrate flashes in my mind. "Is Maggie okay?"

Philip pauses, running a hand through his curls, standing them all up on end. "Did you talk to her?"

"No, I saw she texted me, but I haven't read it yet." I make to move around him, dropping my chocolate on the counter, but he catches me around the waist, pulling me into a hug. "Philip? What's going on? You're scaring me a little."

Immediately, he releases me. "Everything is fine. Well, kind of not. But your sister is fine, and no one is hurt." He corrects himself quickly when I try to move away again. "Um, just don't check your phone until we have a chance to talk."

He takes me by the hand and leads me to the couch, my phone still on the table. "Remember how you couldn't figure out how to tell your family about us?"

"Yeah?"

"They know." Philip grimaces, his shoulders hunching.

Dumbfounded, I don't say anything while my mind races. "Ah, that would explain my phone blowing up."

"You really haven't looked yet?" There's so much concern on Philip's face, I want to say something to ease his worry.

I shrug instead. "No. So tell me how my family knows. And how you know they know. Do they know you know they know? And what exactly do they know?"

"I may have said something along the lines of not knocking you up before I married you while talking to Kel." Philip ducks as I round on him. His hands are up by his shoulders, defending himself from my righteous anger.

"I thought we agreed to ease them into the idea?" My voice is getting higher and higher with each word. "What happened to playing it cool like we discussed?"

He gives me the short version of his morning with Kel and Nate and how Nate was the catalyst for everyone else finding out. There's an undercurrent of tension in him that I've rarely seen, a hint of panic in his eyes that screams I should tread lightly, except I can't. There's a sick, sinking feeling in my stomach, which only gets worse when coupled with the guilt that Philip doesn't know about my interview and is only concerned about what's waiting for me on my phone.

"And here I thought Cassie was going to be the one to spill the beans." My head is in my hands, and I lean over on the couch. My omission is starting to feel more and more like betrayal.

It doesn't matter that, in theory, I knew these conversations were going to happen. That I'd planned to tell both him and Maggie the respective news this afternoon. Being faced with the reality of the confrontation before I planned it has me as sweaty and nervous as Philip.

"Is it really so bad?" he asks, tentatively wrapping an arm around my shoulders. "They were going to find out eventually. Now it's all over, and all we have to do is keep living our life together, like we would have anyway."

"But now they're going to know what a reckless idiot I was." I regret the words as soon as Philip's arm stiffens and he pulls away. "Wait, wait. I'm sorry. I didn't mean that the way it sounded. Reckless and idiot are two different things." I sit up straight, catching his hands in mine, refusing to let him go anywhere. Taking a deep breath, I clamp down on the anxiety that keeps telling me to hide the truth. He has never given me a reason to doubt I'm important to him. Confessing my feelings, and my shortcomings, isn't going to make him suddenly leave. Even if the rampant emotions vibrating through his body hint that it just might.

I take a deep breath to steady myself. "Reckless was getting married in Vegas as a form of immigration control. The idiot part was that it took me two years to realize I've been in love with you this whole time, and everyone knew except me." I keep my eyes on him, hoping he can see the truth in my words.

Crinkles form at the corner of his eyes as he smiles at me, the tension leaving as quickly as it came. "Everyone except *us*, you mean."

This man. How could I have doubted him when he has never been anything but supportive? "I have to tell you something." I cringe as his eyes narrow and he starts to pull away. "I had an interview this morning. That's why I came home."

Philip's expression turns confused and the pit reappears in my belly. "Okay...why do you sound like you're confessing a deep, dark secret? An interview is good news, isn't it?"

"It is." The fuzzy cushion at my back is itchy; that must be the reason I keep squirming. "It's just that the job is based in South Carolina. And it's not remote."

My husband leans back, making space between us as he stares me down. "That's what Cassie was talking about?" He pulls a hand down his face, scrubbing at his cheeks. "I don't understand why you didn't tell me about it sooner, liefling."

The nerves coiling in my gut at the uncertainty in his voice twist tighter. I have to tell him—he deserves the whole truth. "That's not all. She offered me the job."

The silence at my confession is so tense I can hear my neighbor's car door slam outside. Do I break it? Why isn't he talking? I depend on him to know what to say to fill the quiet. I have no practice at being the yapper.

Finally, he breaks. "Are you going to take it?"

I don't know what I was expecting him to say, but the blunt question was not it. Startled, I say the only thing that pops into my mind. "Should I?"

"Why are you asking me now, if my opinion didn't matter before the interview?" He pushes off the couch, pacing to the window and back. His back is to me, but the tension in his shoulders is clear.

The highs and lows of this conversation are coming faster and faster. And I've always hated roller coasters.

My next words come out small, the guilt at his hurt weighing them down in my throat. "Are you upset? You didn't tell me about the job in Australia." I pull the fuzzy pillow from behind me and hold it to my stomach, curling over it, holding myself together while Philip paces the room, looking anywhere but at me.

Finally, he stops, rounding on me. "A job I wasn't actually going to take. Because I didn't want to leave *you*." He throws his hands up in the air, then resumes pacing. "I just. I thought we told each other everything. What other secrets have you been keeping from me? Anything else Cassie knows that I don't?"

"I wasn't trying to keep it a secret."

If the hurt wasn't written all over his face, I'd giggle at how his curls are standing up all over from the way he's been pulling at them. Instead, I bite back tears as he speaks again, my heart being pulled apart at his reaction. He's so upset, more than I would expect from the situation, and I can't understand why.

I've seen him upset before—seen the thunderclouds build on his face and then dissipate again faster than I could react. But this *is* different. Bigger. A hurricane compared to his usual tempests.

"You did a rather good job of it, though." He sits down on the couch, leaving a gap that might as well be the Grand Canyon between us. "I can't believe you didn't say anything after the other night. I thought we were on the same page."

"We are on the same page, Philip."

He doesn't resist when I take his hand, but he doesn't lace his fingers through mine like I hoped. Instead, he looks at me like I'm a stranger, sending a dagger through me.

"Are we?"

Another painful silence smothers us. One that I think I have to be the one to break. Only I don't know how. I don't know what to say to make it better when I don't know what's broken in the first place. How did everything fall apart so fast?

The silence stretches on longer and longer, until I drop his hand and snap. "Tell me how to fix this. What are you thinking?"

He doesn't answer. Hands dangling between his knees and head bowed, my husband shakes his head, before pushing back up to his feet. "I need a minute."

I swipe for his hand but miss, grasping empty air instead. "Wait, please. I don't—" I choke on my words as I follow him to the front door. "What happened? Tell me what's wrong, please. I don't understand how we got here. I thought everything was fine, was good, between us?"

Philip doesn't turn around, but he stops in the doorway, his hands braced on either side, heat hitting me full in the chest, adding to my burning confusion and pain. "What else don't I know? What else haven't we discussed? A day ago, I would have said I know everything about you. Now I'm realizing that I don't. Do you want kids? A dog? A cat?"

When I don't answer immediately, too shocked by the turn this conversation has taken, he turns, eyes glassy as he stares me down. "Would you have left me behind and moved? Moved on?"

"No, I..." I barely get the words out before he steps back. "You do know me. You know me better than anyone else, I promise."

"It doesn't feel like it."

My heart matches each step he takes, beating as slowly as an executioner's march. When he walks away, I don't follow.

Philip

IT TAKES ME EXACTLY one hundred and ninety-two steps to realize that I'm an ass.

That's how long it takes before Jono answers his phone with a worried, "Flip? Is this about the job? Because I just heard there's a new hire joining next week, and if that's you and you haven't told me, I'm going to be right pissed. And if it's not you, that's good news because the poor sap is going to be working under George, and he's a knob head."

"I think I've made a mistake." My confession is out before I stop my feet. Blinded by my angst, I'd wandered away from Ophie's house, following the sidewalk through the complex. Finding myself on a greenbelt, I keep going while I sort out my thoughts.

The cloud of confusion and hurt that had made it impossible to stay inside and keep talking to Ophie dissipated the second the sun warmed my skin. Once again, the mood swings I've tried so hard to control got the better of me. Now I have a mess to clean up. But first, I need some sense smacked into me, courtesy of my brother.

"Well, that's not news. What have you done now?" Jono asks, the tapping of his keyboard barely audible.

There's an unoccupied bench just to my right. Changing directions, I head for it. "Ophie and I got into a bit of a row, and I think it's my fault."

"Again, that's not exactly new, is it?"

"I suppose not. But I think I've really done it this time." The bench is hot enough to burn the back of my legs as I sit, but I ignore it in favor of getting advice with minimal fuss.

Clearing my throat, I get the worst shock over with first. "So, for starters, you should know that Ophelia and I kind of got married."

"Kind of married? You're either married or you're not, boetie."

"We got all-the-way, legally married." I choke back a laugh. Trust Jono to give me shit, even when I'm feeling low.

"Well, congratulations. Or is that the mistake? I thought Ophelia was great? She's been awesome every time I've talked to her." Paper rustles in the background, and Jono calls out something to someone I can't make out. "I assume you're staying in the States, then?"

"For now. But we had a bit of a...I don't want to say fight. More like, she told me something I didn't want to hear, and I think I may have overreacted." I outline the conversation and how it had gone from both of us accidentally spilling the beans to me storming out after being blindsided by the news of her job offer.

There's a long scratch in the plastic material of the bench, the rough edge of it distracting me from my frayed feelings as I run my finger over it.

"What were you really upset about, then? People figuring out your not-very-well-kept secret? Or Ophie getting a job offer when you haven't? Or am I missing something?" It's annoying how quickly my brother can lay out all the reasons I feel like crap.

"What if she takes the job and leaves me behind?" The fear that she'll leave me adrift makes my well-thought-out argument sound more like a whine.

"Is that a real question?"

Hiking one foot up onto the bench, I lean my elbow against my knee so I can mope more easily. "Maybe."

"God, you're an idiot sometimes." Jono snorts into the phone. "Did you or did you not get married?"

"Yes." A squirrel runs along the branch of a tree across the patch of grass, holding something in his teeth. Even the wildlife has a job, unlike me. Right, maybe Jono has a bit of a point.

"And you're not taking the job here because you don't want to leave Ophie, right?"

"Right." The squirrel stops to stare at me. Judging me.

Jono sighs into the phone. A familiar sound. "And she hasn't actually taken the job yet, as she *just* got the offer. And immediately told you?"

Right. It appears I have, in fact, overreacted. "I see where you're going with this. I'm not prepared to say you're right, but I can't argue that you're wrong."

"Didn't those vows mean that you guys were going to figure it out together? Wasn't there some line in there about 'hard times and good'?"

"Actually, I think it was 'I promise never to step on your blue suede shoes,' but I get the point you're making."

"So figure it out together."

"Figure what out?"

"Life, you dummy."

I don't need a video to know that Jono is shaking his head and rolling his eyes at me right now.

"Do you think I just decided one day to move to Australia? Nicola and I talked it out. With words. We made a freaking spreadsheet. Like adults. Because adults make decisions that way. Especially married ones. Now quit being an idiot, go apologize, and talk it out with your *wife*."

"God, you're bossy." I give him the middle finger, not that he can see it, a smile tugging at the corners of my mouth.

"And Flippy?"

I pull the phone back to my ear. "Yeah?"

"Tell Ophie congrats from us. And that I'm sorry I inherited all the good genes and left you with all the idiot ones."

Ophie

STICKING MY HEAD IN the freezer not only sends a wave of deliciously cold air over my face and shoulders but also helps to keep in check the tears threatening to escape. Damn Philip for ruining what should have been an exciting moment.

Also, why don't I have any ice cream? I could have sworn I had some stashed in here for emergencies. And I am pretty sure that my best friend, my husband, not being immediately happy for me when I get the job offer of a lifetime counts as an emergency.

Goddammit, I bet Maggie and Kel ate it. I refuse to follow that train of thought any further and step back, closing the freezer door. Instead of diving into a creamy tub of feel-good, I pour myself a glass of water. Unsatisfying, but better than nothing.

My fingers shake as I set the glass down, an involuntary whimper accompanying the breath I blow out with it. I won't cry. I won't. Even though every part of me wants to run outside after him, I refuse to.

After three years of staying stubbornly single, I've been in a real relationship for forty-eight hours and am already tempted to give up everything in order to make a man feel better about himself. Two years as my best friend, and I really thought I knew Philip better than that, thought he would never ask me to mold myself to him.

Maybe I was wrong.

When he hasn't come back after five minutes, the realization that this is one of those rare times he's not going to bounce back immediately settles over me. Fuck.

Fighting the churning feeling inside me, I snuggle into the couch and flip on the TV. Picking up my phone, I start scrolling through the dozens of messages. It only takes reading the first few texts to reassure myself that the only emergency is that my family has figured out I actually don't have it all together, and maybe I'm more like Maggie than they realized.

Instead of responding, I toss my phone down so I can pretend everything is fine. I'm well into being distracted by a trash reality show with *Love* in the title when the front door bursts open. Heart pounding, I stay put, staring at the large bouquet of flowers, half dozen balloons, and heavy grocery bag in Philip's arms.

"I am so sorry, liefling" are the first words out of his mouth. His hair is standing up on end, the opposite of his drooping shoulders and sad expression. "I am so proud of you and want to hear all about the job."

I haven't moved from the couch, my legs still tucked up beneath me, a pillow crushed to my stomach, as he stands there, chest heaving like he's run a marathon. "What made you change your mind?" A reciprocal apology is fighting its way out of me, but I clamp my teeth and keep it inside. This isn't about who was right or wrong. It's about me knowing my husband is going to celebrate my success without seeing it as an attack on his.

Philip sets the grocery bag down and crosses to the couch, laying the flowers on the coffee table in front of me. "It took about a minute of me acting like a baby to realize that you weren't threatening to leave me behind." He rubs a hand to the back of his neck, whistling under his breath. "You hadn't even said you were going to take the job, I just assumed. And you know what happens when you assume."

At the reminder of our favorite professor's favorite saying, a tiny smile cracks my lips. "This time, I think it only made an ass of you, babe."

Gently, he takes the pillow away from me, then pulls me into his lap. The forgotten balloons bounce against the low ceiling, dangling strings in our faces. I flap at them, sputtering as they tickle my nose, until Philip snags them and coaxes the balloons away from us.

"Liefling. Can you forgive me for being a baboon? I want to hear all about the job and how badass my wife is going to be." He plants a kiss on my forehead as I settle into his arms.

"God, it's so hard to stay mad at you."

"I was hoping you would say that."

Not ready to give in yet, I kick at the bag on the floor before looking at him with a question in my eyes. "What's in the bag?"

"Ice cream." He kisses my temple. "Sour gummies." My cheek. "Chocolate." His lips meet the corner of my mouth. "String cheese." His lips press into mine as I grin against the kiss.

Pinching his chin, I pull back so I can study his face. "What flavor ice cream?"

He smirks back. "Spumoni."

Slithering off his lap, I snag the bag off the floor before taking it to the kitchen. "You really do know the way to buy my forgiveness." I pull out a bowl and the ice cream scoop. When I look over, he's watching me with hopeful eyes. "None for you. I'm not sharing my bribe."

He laughs while I dish out a generous serving, then bring it and myself back to the couch. He makes to pull me back onto his lap, but I sidestep and settle in the chair beside him. "You'll steal a bite."

Holding up his hands, he laughs before gesturing for me to speak. Between bites, I fill him in on Penny Zimmerman and her company and the very well-paid position she just offered me. He asks thoughtful questions and cheers for me at all the right moments, breaking down the last bit of resentment I'd been harboring.

"If the benefits package is everything she promised, you'd be crazy not to take this job," he says as I finish. "When did she say she would email it?" He looks so lonely over there on the couch, and an irresistible pull draws me to him.

I settle beside him, sighing as his arm drops over my shoulder to pull me close. "By the end of the week. You really think I should take it? You're not just saying that because we got in a fight about it?"

Tucking a strand of hair behind my ear so he can press a kiss to the side of my head, he chuckles. "Obviously, I think you should wait for the official offer and see what it says, but yeah. I'll go anywhere you go. Heck, I'll be your stay-at-home husband if it's generous enough. I could be a lady who lunches."

"Speaking of ladies who lunch." I dig my phone out from beneath my calves. "Want to know the damage?" With a sigh, I swipe open my phone. "Seven missed calls from Maggie, one from Daisy, and three from my mother."

Philip groans. "And how many texts?"

I pull up my messages. "Too many. From all of them. Even Kel." Sighing, I snuggle back into the crook of his arm on the couch. "Maybe we only read the highlights?"

He leans over to kiss the top of my head. "Just the highlights."

I scan the screen. Should I start with the individual texts from my family or the group chat that's still going? I tap Maggie's, since she's the instigator of all of this, and start reading out loud.

"Ophie, why did Kel just ask me how long you and Philip have been sleeping together? And why is this news to me?" Further down the page, another message catches my eye. "'Have you been together this whole time and none of us noticed?' Oh, here's another good one. 'Is it the accent? It's the accent, isn't it? It makes him sound so proper, even when he's talking complete bullshit.'"

Philip laughs at that one. "Does it?"

"It does." I poke his side. "Americans are suckers for an English accent, and yours is particularly nice to listen to."

Her next text has heat running up my cheeks, but I don't share it with Philip.

Mags: Does he talk dirty to you in that accent? I bet that is so hot. I don't actually want an answer to that one because I don't want to think of my future brother-in-law having sex with my sister, but still. It's hot, isn't it?

Mags: OMG, is that where you've been going when Kel and I are at the house? To have sex with him?

Mags: OMG, is that WHY you've been going??????? Do I make loud sex noises?!?!?!?

Mags: Well, Kel is now rolling on the floor laughing (literally) because he said that's how he put two and two together. Nate said we're both loud?!?! I am MORTIFIED!

Mags: Do you think Daisy is loud too? Is it a Moore sister thing? What a weird thing for us all to have in common. I don't know if I'll be able to keep a straight face the next time I see Daisy. The visual in my head...make it stop!

Mags: This is all your fault. I have to go bleach my brain now.

"I wonder if being loud during sex is a matter of nature vs. nurture?" Philip laughs, his chin digging into my shoulder as he reads Maggie's messages. "Or maybe it's just because all three of you jabber like a bunch of baboons."

"Hmph. You talk way more than I do. And that is the last time we are ever going to talk about how much noise my sisters and I make during sex." I lock my screen and shove my phone underneath the throw pillows beside me. "It's probably better than what Daisy and my mom are going to say."

I lean my head against Philip's chest, taking a moment to focus on the sound of his heart beating beneath my ear. It's slow and steady. Dependable. Philip may love a good joke and never take anything seriously, but the one thing he has always been is dependable.

"What does *your* family think?" Anything to delay the moment of judgment by a few more minutes. "Did you already tell them?"

Philip hands me his phone, the screen unlocked, to show me the WhatsApp conversation between his family.

Nicola: *Does this mean Mum and I are going to be slightly less outnumbered? Can't wait to welcome her officially.*

Jono: *Poor girl. Does she know what she's got herself into?*

Mum: *When can we meet her in person? Does this mean you're going to come visit soon?*

Dad: *Can't say I'm surprised, but congratulations, son. Hopefully she's a bit more sensible than you.*

"Is it bad that I'm annoyed at your dad's attitude? I'm not sure what's worse—my family thinking I've lost my mind or yours not being surprised at all that you'd do something like this?" Bolstered by my anger, I release my phone from time out and unlock it.

Philip puts a hand over mine before I can read anything. "My family loves me. Do they think I'm flighty and unserious? Absolutely—it's also true. But I know that they would do anything for me if I asked, so I don't mind the ribbing."

He presses a kiss to the side of my head, and a warm fuzzy works its way down my spine, easing the tension knotting my stomach. "Your family loves you too. You've always acted with a high standard of having your shit together. Are they going to be surprised? I'm sure. Will they question your sanity? Very likely. But it won't make them love you any less, liefling."

"I still can't believe I never asked you what that word meant before."

"For the last year and a half, I've been waiting for you to ask. Or look it up on your own and show up ready to disabuse me of my fantasy."

"Pretty sure I've been living on a river in Egypt."

Philip scrunches his face, groaning. "That was so bad."

I bend at the waist, awkwardly trying to bow from my position beside him on the couch. "I'll be here all week, ladies and gentlemen." I slither to the floor, phone still in hand. "Ready?"

Daisy: *You didn't seriously MARRY Philip, did you? What were you thinking? Are you even thinking about your future? Did you get knocked up? You know there's other options than marrying him, right?*

Mom: *This is very unexpected, Ophelia. Are you sure that's a good idea?*

Trust Daisy to be the one who makes me feel the worst. I should have expected no less, but my mom's message is less judgmental than I expected, and her follow-up message makes me feel even better about the whole thing.

Mom: *Philip is really a lovely young man, though. Maybe more of a flibbertigibbet than I would have picked for you. But if you're happy, then I'm happy for you, sweetie. Maybe we can have a small reception or something?*

"We're a pair of dummies, aren't we?" Philip leans forward, resting his forehead against mine. "You're not angry with me?"

I shake my head ever so slightly. "No, dummy, I forgave you the second you walked in the door with my favorite ice cream flavor. I'm just not looking forward to the deluge of questions we're about to face." Now I pull back, meeting his eyes once more. "You ready, Mr. Moore?"

He grins. "Technically, not Mr. Moore. But yeah. Let's do it."

Epilogue

OPHIE'S EYES KEEP CLOSING as we shuffle forward in line. My back aches from being squished in an airplane seat for hours and hours, but at least I managed to sleep for a good chunk of the flight from Los Angeles to Sydney. I suppose having the window seat and both of our winter coats for pillows helped. Unlike my wife, who apparently didn't sleep longer than an hour at a time over the course of our fifteen-hour flight.

Now she's nodding off every time we pause, only waking up to shuffle forward a few steps. "Liefling, we're almost to the front." I kiss the top of her head to wake her up. The smell of her shampoo is faint, and I can definitely smell the almost twenty-four hours of travel on her, but I don't care. I'm sure I could use a shower just as badly.

And a nap.

I would kill to be horizontal right now. Instead, I hand our passports to the immigration control officer at Sydney International and answer her questions before steering us to baggage claim. Ophie is silent, her eyes drooping and shoulders slumping as we wait.

Last Christmas, our first married, we stayed in South Carolina, enjoying each other. Ophelia was working crazy hours as Zimmerman ramped up for the holidays, and I was still waiting to do my visa interview.

Sutton's friend Alfie hired me to help him with his headhunting business and offered to sponsor me for an H-1B visa. Besides, we didn't want to leave our new addition to the family.

But this year, we left our greyhound rescue, Daphne, with a friend and finally managed to come see my family with my shiny new American green card in hand.

"Almost there, love." I wrap an arm around her waist, letting her lean against me. Sweat pricks along my spine as summer sunshine pours in through the skylights above us.

"I want to be so mad at you for actually sleeping on the plane. But you looked so uncomfortable, I didn't have the heart." Ophie sighs as she snuggles into my side. "I didn't think it was possible to sleep with your head at that angle. Are you sure your neck is okay?" She runs a hand up my spine, pressing between my shoulder blades, and I stifle an inappropriate groan at the pressure.

"I'll be fine once I get a nap." I mirror her, digging my thumb into the base of her spine, just above the waistband of her sweatpants. Before she can do more than flutter her eyes closed, her bright yellow suitcase comes down the conveyor, and I jump forward to snatch it up. I hand it off to her as my matching suitcase follows a few seconds later.

"Ready?" I grab the handle and march us off to the restrooms. "Are they in my case or yours?"

"Mine. Give me one second, and I'll pull them out." Ophie grins as we move out of the foot traffic. Kneeling down, she unzips her suitcase, then pulls out a neon tie-dye T-shirt and hands it to me. Even if this weren't going to be an epic prank, I'm eager to swap my East Coast winter gear for summer togs. She pulls out a matching cotton dress for herself before zipping it back up. "Meet you back here in five?"

I lean down to kiss her before she pulls back, making a face. "I'm going to brush my teeth. I can smell myself." She laughs, then shoves me toward the men's room.

Shirt changed, teeth brushed, and armpits refreshed, I wait for her in front of the women's loo, spinning my suitcase on its wheels as I wait. An older couple shakes their head at me as they pass through to customs. I grin back, knowing they read my shirt.

So what if the joke is two years old? Pee-pee jokes are never not funny.

Ophie emerges from the bathroom, her dark hair freshly pulled back into a thick braid and looking much more awake than before. The cotton dress pulls across her chest, tempting me as always. The same bubble letters are splashed across the front, although hers spell out "Auntie Pee-Pee" instead of "Unca Pee-Pee" like mine.

She kneels down and shoves the clothing in her hand into the suitcase. "Let me just change my shoes quickly." She swaps her trainers and socks for a pair of sandals. I don't dare after my feet have been trapped inside my own trainers for so long.

"Ready?" I hold out my hand, and Ophie takes it.

"I cannot believe I let you talk me into this." She shakes her head at me. "Let the record show just how much I love you."

I pull her against my chest, resting my chin on top of her head as her arms wrap behind my back. "Talk you into this? I believe the whole thing was your idea, Mrs. van der Merwe." Ophie grunts and buries her face deeper into my chest. "And let the record show just how much it means to me that you're willing to be in on the joke."

In the two years we've been officially married, Ophie has not only tolerated my jokes, but she's started suggesting her own, much to my delight. I'll never admit it out loud, but sometimes her suggestions are funnier than mine.

Auntie Pee-Pee.

My nephews are gonna love it, and Jono is going to hate it, which is perfect.

"Let's go, Mr. Moore. Before I fall asleep on my feet." She tugs me toward customs and through the "nothing to declare" line.

"Flip!"

I hear my brother before I see him, waving his arms overhead. We head toward them, waving and grinning as we weave through the press of bodies.

Mum and Dad are standing next to him, Mum's curly hair finer than I remember, but otherwise, they look sun-kissed and healthy. Jono drags a hand down his face as we get close enough for him to take in our clothes. "Are you serious?"

Ophie and I laugh as Jono and Dad groan. Mum is too busy hugging Ophie to notice. I'm swept up in a hug as soon as she releases my wife. "Oh, Flip. Oh, my boy, I'm so glad to see you." She babbles away as she squeezes my ribs. "And Ophelia, I can't believe you're here."

Mum releases me so Jono can get in a hug. The two of us are passed between the three of them for multiple rounds of hugs before we manage to get sorted with bags and cases, and then Jono leads the way out of the terminal.

The car is filled with chatter as we drive back to Jono and Nicola's house, where she and the boys are waiting for us. Ophie squeezes in the middle between Mum and me in the back, answering every question Mum throws her way with a tired smile. They let us go ahead when we arrive, insisting they can bring the bags inside for us.

I take Ophie's hand as we walk up the front steps and knock on the door. "Ready?"

"Always." She goes up on her toes and plants a minty-fresh kiss on my lips as the front door opens.

"Gross!"

"Ew!"

"Awww!"

My nephews and sister-in-law all exclaim at once as we separate. Ophie and I turn to face them at the same time, and Nicola bursts out laughing. Davy a second behind her, shrieking with laughter as he sees the shirts.

I can't wait to see their faces when they open the matching ones we got for the whole family.

This is going to be the best Christmas ever.

Want to meet the owners of Sunshine Cellars and see where it all began? Keep reading for a sneak peek of *Bastard-in-Chief*!

Or, use the QR code below to sign up for my newsletter and get a free short story, plus stay in the know on all things Fancy!

Acknowledgements

This book was a bit of a solo endeavor until the end. I'm not sure what made me keep this one so close to the chest while writing it, but Ophie and Philip really wanted to stay a secret right up until the end.

Y'all, I don't know why Brooklyn puts up with me, but the woman deserves a million dollars a year for the way she keeps me on track. I can't afford to pay her that much, so I'm paying her in book boyfriends and Crumbl cookies instead.

Ophelia Moore is made up of all those "shoulds" we pile on our plates. All the ways we want to put on a show of having it together, that we're not just a collection of fears and desires held together with duct tape and ibuprofen. I love the way she desperately wants to keep her shit together, but can't fight the way Philip makes her feel safe enough to be a little messy.

My bestie jokes that she's going to have to put a leash on me when we get old. But the truth is, my brain turns off a little when we're together, because I trust her to have my back. And she will blindly follow me through a parking lot because she always assumes I know where I'm going. Find your person and hold them close, even when they get a little derpy.

May we all find someone who lets us be a little messy.

Bastard-in-Chief

THE SCENT OF FRESH tortillas hits my nose the moment I follow my best friend through the door of our favorite downtown restaurant. "But what about Emma?"

"Sophie Alexander, it's your thirty-fucking-fifth birthday. You got your divorce papers yesterday. We are going out to get plastered on lethal margaritas tonight to celebrate your freedom from Teeny Peeny *and* you reaching your sexual prime. I already texted Emma, she's spending the night at Bella's house." She shakes her head at me before I can protest, her chin-length hair swinging. "And no, she didn't want to come, I already asked. No normal fifteen-year-old wants to hang out with her mom on a Friday night."

"Happy Birthday, Sophie!" A large table of women greets us as we make our way deeper into the restaurant from the bar. Jess raises her glass in a toast, her margarita already half drunk.

Lauren pushes me into the booth with Jess and a few other ladies from work. I don't know most of them, but I smile anyway. Angela from Marketing slides a margarita to me with a birthday greeting. I take a sip that burns on the way down, as lethal as advertised.

I join in the meaningless chatter while I drink, letting the tequila warm me from the inside. One of the girls from accounting is in the middle of a story about her latest blind date when Jess squeaks, clutching at my arm.

"Oh. My. God." Her nails dig painfully into my upper arm. "Is that Theodore-fuck-me-Sutton?"

"What?" I crane my neck to catch a glimpse. Shit. There he is. The quintessential grumpy boss we all work for is leaning on the bar, sipping from a glass of golden liquid. I'm pretty sure the whole table sighs out loud watching his Adam's apple bob as he swallows.

Everyone in the office is terrified of him, but that doesn't mean he isn't the subject of more than one secret fantasy.

Like the novel I've been writing.

The one that features a hero with dark looks like his, and a gruff exterior.

"Soph!" Lauren snaps a finger in front of my face. "Time for presents!" She shoves a hot pink gift bag into my hands.

"Thanks, babe." I move to tuck the bag under my chair, next to my purse, but Lauren grabs it.

"Nope, you have to open it now. I need to see your face!" She grins at me, the same grin that got us into trouble on more than one occasion in college.

"Lauren..." I give her a warning look before reaching in and pulling out a pink envelope. "Pink? Really?"

Lauren just laughs. "It's a theme. Open it already!"

I take my time reading the card to annoy her, smiling at her use of the nicknames we gave each other back in college.

Bitch,

Have I told you lately how proud of you I am? You already know how I feel about Jake and his actions, but I am so excited to see you finally putting yourself first. Here's a little something so you can keep pursuing the things that you love, and so you can take care of yourself. Love you!

- Slut

"Aww, thanks babe." Laughing, I wipe my eyes before pulling the first tissue-wrapped shape out of the bag. "Hmm, this feels like a book. Always a good choice." Ripping off the paper reveals a stack of three books—Lucy Score's newest, a signed copy of one of Annette Marie's *Demonized* books for my collection, and a craft book called *Romancing the Beat.*

"So you can finally finish that book instead of spending all your free time writing boring articles for me." Lauren grins at me. "You know I'm dying to read more. You left me hanging at chapter six and I neeeeeeeed to know if they fuck."

She's not wrong. Answering the phones and directing traffic at Mailbox, Inc is just one of the jobs I do to pay the bills. What no one besides Lauren knows, is that I write articles for the company blog under a pen name for extra money.

When Mr. Sutton instructed Lauren to add a blog to Mailbox's website, posting articles about business and technology in order to increase Mailbox's visibility, she was able to hire "Elinor Price" without fuss. Lauren's also the only person who knows that there's a series of unfinished romance novels burning a hole in the hard drive of my laptop at home.

Jake, my ex-husband, hated my love of romances. It should have been a sign.

"These are amazing, thank you." I give her a sideways hug.

"Oh, that's just the start. That was your official birthday gift. Now you have to open your 'Happy Divorce' gift."

"Is it decent for the public? Your face is twitching."

Lauren laughs, taking another long sip of her margarita. "Probably not, but open it anyway. We never got to have a bachelorette party for you since you were already pregnant with Emma and your courthouse wedding didn't let me celebrate my bestie the way she deserves."

Needing to steel myself for whatever it is she's wrapped in here, I take a long draw on my drink for some tequila courage. The weight of the bag gives me no clue what it could be. "I love you and I hate you."

"Hate-love you too, Soph." She winks. "Quit stalling and open the damn gift."

I pull out the first package, stripping the tissue paper from it before Lauren can say anything else. "Lipstick?" I hold up the tube to examine it in the dim light of the restaurant. The black case looks expensive, though I don't recognize the gold "KB" stamped on it. It's a good gift, I never buy myself expensive makeup.

"Nope." Lauren grins. "Take off the cap."

I pull the cap off to reveal a hot pink silicone tip. "Oh my God...is that?" I slam the cap back on, my cheeks burning. "Lauren!" I hiss. "Is that a fucking *vibrator*?"

"That's not even the best part." Lauren is in hysterics. "Open the next one." She grabs at the bag, intending to pull it out for me.

"Is it a dildo? Tell me it's not a fucking dildo, Lauren. I am *not* opening a dildo in public." I glance around wildly catching Mr. Sutton still at the bar. Is he waiting for someone? "Especially where our *boss* could see it."

"Don't be a party pooper, he's not even paying attention to us. Like Theodore Sutton would ever deign to pay attention to the peons. He's probably just waiting for a to-go order."

Nervous, I unwrap the second gift. It's small and square so at least I know I'm not about to end up waving a giant penis in the air. Pulling off the paper reveals a black jewelry box. I crack open the lid. Inside is a gold ring, one of those big statement ones, the quartz-crystal shaped top bold and exciting. Too bad I'm not bold or exciting enough to pull it off.

"Wow. Thanks, Lauren. It's gorgeous." It is, it really is, I'm just not cool enough to wear it myself. I pull it out of the box and slip it on the middle finger of my right hand, the ring long enough to cover my entire knuckle. This is the kind of thing Lauren would wear to work. The only ring I've ever worn was my wedding ring, the plain silver band all Jake and I could afford when we got married at twenty. He never bought me anything else—not that we would have had the money for it even if he'd bothered.

The weight of it on my right hand is as unfamiliar as the emptiness of my left ring finger. The more I stare at it, the more I'm convinced I've seen her wearing this exact ring. "Isn't this almost exactly like the one you have?"

A mischievous grin sneaks across Lauren's face. "It's *exactly* like the one I have. It has a secret." She pulls my hand toward her and slips the ring off my finger. "See this little circle?" She points to a button I hadn't noticed on the underside of the decorative shape. "Tap it."

I do, shrieking and nearly dropping it when the whole thing starts buzzing in the palm of my hand. Jess and the other girls at the table demand to see so it gets passed around, while I take a deep breath and try not to throttle my best friend. She took me and Emma in when I left Jake, I can't kill her over a vibrator ring.

Shit. Is Sutton still here? I turn to look at the bar, praying that he's left already. Instead, I find myself looking straight into his eyes, his long fingers wrapped around a sweating glass. He doesn't look away. Just stares me down, those fathomless blue eyes locked on mine, ice cubes clinking as he swirls his drink. Goosebumps prickle under the sleeve of my cardigan, and my heart speeds up.

"Isn't it the greatest? Perfect for the discreet pick-me-up when it's been a rough day at work." When I don't respond, Lauren pokes me in the side, breaking the spell Sutton has me under. "When was the last time you had an orgasm, Soph? I know you wouldn't go on a date until the divorce was official, and the papers only came yesterday."

If it was possible for my cheeks to get any hotter, I'd give myself second-degree burns. "Two years," I mumble under my breath.

"Two years? Did you seriously just say you haven't had an orgasm in two years?"

I clap my hand over her mouth. Lauren's voice is loud enough to hear clear across the room. She wrenches free from my grasp. "Woman! How are you even alive? Also, you've only been separated for nine months. Are you telling me that Jake left you hanging high and dry for over a year while you were still together?"

"For God's sake, Lauren, keep your voice down." I will myself not to glance around. If I don't look, I won't know if Mr. Sutton is listening to this conversation. Living in denial is better than certain death by embarrassment if I turn and he's looking. Emma needs me, I can't die now.

As Lauren keeps talking, the conversation turns to all the ways my ex-husband did me wrong. Starting with the lack of orgasms, continuing to how he spent money we didn't have, and ending with the whole "sleeping with one of his model friends" that ultimately led to our divorce. I don't have the energy to interrupt so I focus on not turning around to look for Sutton.

A flash of movement in the mirror along the wall to my right catches my eye. Sutton is taking a to-go bag from one of the hostesses. I can't help watching as he pulls his wallet out of his pocket, the movement pushing his jacket aside and revealing the fact that the man doesn't skip leg day at the gym. Dragging my eyes up his body, I take the opportunity to ogle to my heart's content, the alcohol in my belly telling me it's a fantastic idea.

My gaze finishes by tracing the strong line of his jaw, a tequila-flavored voice in the back of my head wondering what it would feel like to run my tongue along it, or what that stubble would feel like against my skin.

"Shit. Sutton is staring at you, Sophie." Jess's voice cuts through my fantasy, jarring me back to reality.

I meet his eyes and all the air leaves my lungs. He holds my gaze for a moment before tipping his chin an inch, one dark eyebrow lifting with the action, grabbing his order and walking out the door.

Fuck. Me.

About Author

Fancy Roberts likes her heroes how she likes her coffee—hot, strong, and at least twice a day. Classy on the outside, and sassy on the inside, Fancy loves nothing more than to drop a well-timed profanity and tell a sexy story.

Just like her, Fancy's heroines are more than meets the eye and give as good as they get. The road to their happily ever after may be rocky, but she promises everyone gets what they deserve in the end.

Besides, who doesn't love a woman who orders a whiskey, neat, then tells you a dirty joke while wearing a twinset and pearls?

Also By Fancy Roberts

Mailbox, Inc series

Bastard-in-Chief

Chief-of-Security

Editor-in-Chief

Sunshine Cellars

Pinot Promises

Merlot Marriage

Sunshine Cellars #3 coming in 2025!

www.ingramcontent.com/pod-product-compliance
Lightning Source LLC
Chambersburg PA
CBHW072007210726
48294CB00013B/1718